THE BOOK OF LARK AND MOLE

ERIC MARDER

ISBN-10: 1478166304
EAN-13: 9781478166306

Library of Congress Control Number: 2012911923
CreateSpace Independent Publishing Platform
North Charleston, SC

Contents

1. The Magic Pen

When they were children, Mole and Lark were best friends. They did things together and played together. But when they grew up, they forgot that they had been friends once. They still lived in the same town, but they no longer did things together.

Mole was a shoemaker. People came to his store. He asked them to stand on a piece of cardboard, and he drew the outline of their feet. He used the drawing on the cardboard to cut leather for the soles of the shoes, so the shoes would fit perfectly. The soles were made of four layers of hard leather which were glued together. This made the soles of the shoes very strong. The upper parts of the shoes were made of soft leather. This made the shoes very comfortable. All of his customers liked the shoes Mole made for them. He was a good shoemaker.

Lark was a poet. Once a week or twice a week, he wrote a new poem. Some of his poems had rhymes. Some didn't. Some were happy and made you want to laugh. Some were sad and made you want to cry. Some were about things that happened in the town. Some were about far-away places. But something about the words in the poems always surprised you. The words were put together in such a way that it felt good to hear them. You always wanted to hear more.

Right in the middle of the town, there was an open square with many important buildings around it. The city hall was there with the mayor's office. The museum was there, and a restaurant, and an art gallery, and the police station, and the theatre, and a church, and a synagogue, and a mosque, and a Buddist temple. One other important place was there, right between the theatre and the museum, a place that was just called the "Parlor."

You might think that a place called the Parlor would be just a small room, maybe like a living room. But this wasn't so at all. The Parlor was as large as two gyms. And the entire space was full of round tables and chairs, except for one end which had a long counter. There one could buy desserts -- as many flavors of ice cream as you can imagine; different cakes, pies, cookies; and things to drink, like sodas, coffee, tea, or hot chocolate.

Every evening, many people came to the Parlor. They went to the counter and bought ice cream or other things to eat and drink. Then they found a table where they could sit and talk with their friends.

On most evenings, Lark came to the Parlor. Whenever he had a new poem, he went to the far end of the room. There, three steps led to a small platform . He just stood on the platform, waiting. When people saw him there, they stopped talking. First, just a few people stopped talking. Then more and more people realized that he was there, and they too stopped talking. Finally, the whole room was completely quiet. It was so quiet you could hear people breathing. Then Lark read his latest poem. When he finished, the people clapped. They liked Lark's poems. They thought Lark was a very good poet. They always paid attention to him, and whenever he finished reading a poem, they gathered around him to talk to him.

Mole also came to the Parlor, but no one ever paid attention to him. Mole was too proud to complain. But in his heart he became bitter. "Look at this," he said to himself, "all these people are wearing shoes I made for them, good shoes that fit perfectly. But no one notices me. No one pays attention to me. All they care about is Lark. When he comes in, they get up. They rush to him. They want to talk with him. They want to be with him, because of his poems. But are the poems really his? He never wrote any poems when we were children and played together. Perhaps he just steals the poems from somewhere, so people will pay attention to him."

Mole wanted to get attention just like Lark. Being jealous made him angry, and being angry made him suspicious. So he began to spy on Lark.

One evening, Mole hid outside Lark's house. When Lark came home, Lark turned on the light in his room. Mole looked in through the window and watched. Lark went to his desk and put a large piece of white paper on the desk. He put a pen on top of the paper. Then he went to the other end of the room and sat down in his easy chair. For a while he just sat there quietly. Then he stretched out his arm and pointed at the pen on the desk. Mole was amazed to see that, at the other end of the room, the pen stood up and started to write all by itself. It wrote for a while. Then it stopped and lay down again. When the pen was finished, Lark got up out of his easy chair and walked over to the desk. He picked up the paper and read what the pen had written. Then he nodded to himself, folded the paper, and put it into his pocket. "Aha," Mole said to himself, "I knew it all along. Lark didn't write the poem. He just used magic."

The next time Lark read a poem at the Parlor, and people began to talk about what a good poet Lark was, Mole said, "Maybe Lark didn't really write the poem at all. Maybe he just used magic." But the people just laughed and said, "Don't be silly, Mole. There's no such thing as magic." This made Mole really angry, and when Lark came walking past his table just a little while later, Mole stuck out his leg. Lark tripped, fell on his face, and just lay on the ground. There was blood on the floor. The people gathered around. An ambulance came. Two men lifted Lark on a stretcher and carried him away to take him to the hospital.

No one knew that Mole had tripped Lark, but Mole knew. He had not wanted to hurt Lark. He had just wanted to make Lark look silly, so people would laugh at him. Now Mole felt very bad. He could not sleep all night because he worried about Lark. He prayed for Lark to get well. The very first thing next morning, he went to ask how Lark was. He found out that Lark would have to stay in the hospital for three days, but that he would be all well again at the end of that time.

At first, Mole was happy to hear that his prayer had been answered and that Lark would get better. But as soon as he stopped worrying about Lark, he became jealous again. He thought and thought about it. Finally, he went to Lark's house. He walked around the house and found a window that was open. He climbed in through the window and went to Lark's room. He took the magic pen, put it in his pocket, climbed back out through the window, and went back home again.

That evening, Mole put the pen on top of a piece of paper. He sat down on a chair at the other end of the room. He lifted his arm and pointed at the pen, just as he had seen Lark do. Again the magic pen rose and started to write. Mole waited until the pen had stopped. Then he went over to the desk. The pen had filled the entire page with writing.

Over and over again, it had written: "Shoes, shoes, perfect shoes, I will make perfect shoes."

Mole looked at the paper for a long time. Then he folded it, and put it in his pocket. It was already dark outside, but he went back to Lark's house. The window was still open. He climbed back into the house, put the pen back on the desk from which he had taken it, and left.

When Lark came home from the hospital, he was happy. The doctor in the hospital was a woman named Maya. She had helped him get well in just three days. She was a very good doctor. She had a long dark braid, and now Lark and Maya were going to get married.

Just before the wedding, Mole was sitting at a table in the Parlor when Lark came in. Lark walked toward the rear of the room to read a new poem. When he passed close to Mole's table, Mole got up and said, "I have to tell you something, Lark." But Lark stopped him and said, "No need to tell me, Mole. I know you tripped me, but I'm not mad. You are a good person. Even a good person may sometimes do something bad. But even something bad can sometimes have a good result. If you hadn't tripped me, I wouldn't have gone to the hospital. If I hadn't gone to the hospital, I wouldn't have met Maya. So it turned out well. Do you think we could be friends again like we were when we were small?" And Mole said, "Oh yes, Lark. Oh yes." And Lark hugged Mole, and Mole cried.

Then Lark went to the other end of the room and read his new poem. It was a poem about a beautiful lady with a long dark braid. When he finished, all the people in the room clapped, but Mole clapped the loudest of them all. And a friend of Mole said, "I am surprised that you are clapping. Didn't you say that Lark uses magic?" And Mole said, "I was wrong. There is no magic. But perhaps I was right after all, because Lark is such a good poet. And that is the biggest magic of all."

2. The Threads of Light

Lark and Maya wanted to get married. There are different ways to get married. Some people are married by a clergyman, like a minister, or a priest, or a rabbi, or some other clergyman or clergywoman. Some people are married by a judge. If the people are on a ship in the ocean, they can be married by the captain of the ship. But Lark and Maya were not going to be on a ship, and they did not want to be married by a judge. They did not want to be married by any particular kind of clergyman or clergywoman. They did not want to be married by just one person, not by just a man, not by just a woman. They wanted to be married by two people, a man and a woman.

Outside the town there were mountains. On the side of one of these mountains, halfway up -- which was very high because the mountain was very big – there was a cabin. The cabin was made of big logs of wood. It was a strong cabin. In that cabin lived two people, a man Oaker and his wife Ashly. Lark and Maya wanted to be married by those two people.

Oaker and Ashly were very old and very wise. They knew many things. They knew all about the trees in the forest and the flowers of the field. They knew all about the animals in the forest, squirrels, rabbits, foxes, deer, and bears. They knew all about the insects, bees, ants, grasshoppers, ladybugs, and caterpillars that turn into butterflies when summer comes. They also knew a lot about people and what is in their hearts. Some people in the town said that they could do magic. Lark and Maya were not sure whether they believed this. Maya was a doctor, and doctors believe in science, not magic. Lark was a poet. He thought there might be some magic, like perhaps the magic in poems. But this did not matter. Magic or no magic, they wanted to ask Oaker and Ashly to marry them.

Mole was Lark's friend. He was a shoemaker. When Mole heard that Lark and Maya wanted to go up the mountain, he asked them to come to his store first. He measured their feet. He made a beautiful pair of hiking shoes for Lark, and another beautiful pair of hiking shoes for Maya – hiking shoes that fit perfectly.

Next day, Lark and Maya put on their new hiking shoes. Lark took a backpack, and Maya took a backpack. They took two bottles of water, a loaf of bread, two large pieces of cheese, four oranges, four apples, two packages of peanuts, a bag of pretzels, and a bag of potato chips. This was food for a picnic on the way. They also took warm sweaters, in case it got cold, ponchos that cover the entire body, in case it rained, and blankets one could lie on or wrap oneself in, in case they had to stay outside overnight.

They got up early in the morning, because it was a long hike up to Oaker and Ashly's cabin. At first, they walked on a paved road. Then they walked on a dirt road. At the end of the dirt road, they came to a path that led through a meadow. There were many wild flowers in the meadow. Then they came to trees, a few trees to the left of them and a few trees to the right of them. The path started to lead uphill. There were more and more trees until they were in the forest.

The path got narrower and steeper. At first it was smooth. Then it became rocky. But the hiking shoes Mole had made for them were very good hiking shoes. They were very strong. So Lark and Maya could step on rough edges without losing their balance.

After they had climbed a while, Maya said, "We must stop to drink water." Lark said, "I'm not thirsty." But Maya was a doctor and said, "If we don't drink, we will get dehydrated." This is a word doctors use when the body doesn't have enough water. Water is very important. When a person doesn't have enough water, the person gets weak and sick. So Lark and Maya stopped and drank water from one of the bottles they had brought. Then they continued to climb.

They came to a clearing at the side of the mountain. They spread out their blankets on the grass and made a picnic. Then they went on until they came to a second clearing. This clearing was much higher than the first one. They could look much further into the distance. They could look over the trees and see the town far below. The streets and the buildings of the town looked very small, like toys. They could see the center of the town, the important buildings like the city hall and the museum, and the hospital at the edge of town.

On the other side of the clearing, close to the trees of the forest was Oaker and Ashly's cabin. When Oaker and Ashly saw them, they came to greet them. They did not have visitors very often because it was a long hike to get there.

Lark and Maya knew that both Oaker and Ashly were very old. But they were surprised when they met them. They did not look, or move, or talk the way Lark and Maya expected old people to look and move and talk. Oaker and Ashly were not bent over the way some old people are. They were tall and their bodies were straight. One could see that Oaker was very strong. At the side of the cabin, there was an axe and a pile of wood Oaker had chopped. Ashly had long white hair, all the way down to her waist. It was obvious that she was old, but she was very beautiful.

Lark and Maya explained why they had come. Oaker smiled and looked at Ashly. Ashly smiled and nodded. Then Oaker said. "Yes, we will marry you, but where do you want the wedding to be?" Maya answered, "We don't want to be married in a house. We want to be married outside. We can't be married here, because it is too high to climb for some people. Could we be married on the meadow where the wild flowers are?" "That is a very good idea," said Ashly, "Is there anything special you want us to do or say when we marry you?" Lark and Maya whispered together for a moment. Then Lark answered, "We have come here because we have heard that you are very wise. We are sure that this is so. Marry us any way you think is best. It will bring us good luck. We want to become like you when we get old." Then Oaker said, "Invite your guests. We will come down to the meadow and marry you there with threads of light."

On the wedding day, a large tent was put up on the meadow, in case it rained. But it didn't rain. Many people came. When the wedding started, Lark and Oaker stood on one side of the field. Maya and Ashly stood on the other side. The guests made a big circle around them. Then Oaker put his hand on Lark's arm and started walking. Ashly put her hand on Maya's arm and started walking. They walked until they met in the middle, and Lark and Maya could hold hands.

Oaker asked Lark, "Do you promise to be good to Maya, and help her when she needs help?" And Lark said, "I promise." Ashly asked Maya, "Do you promise to be good to Lark, and help him when he needs help?" And Maya said, "I promise." Oaker touched Lark's chest and Ashly touched Maya's chest. Then Oaker and Ashley touched hands and said together, "We have joined you with many threads of light. You are married now. We hope you will always be healthy and happy." The people cheered and the musicians began to play.

After the wedding, Oaker and Ashly talked with Lark and Maya. Oaker began, "We have married you with threads of light. These threads connect Lark's heart and Maya's heart. The threads are woven into a braid, like a girl's hair. If there are many threads, the braid is thick. If there are few threads, the braid is thin." Ashly said, "You can go on a far-away trip and the threads will still be there. You can pass your hand right through them, and the threads will still be there. You can't break them with your hands, but..." Ashly stopped. All of them were quiet. Then Oaker spoke softly, "You can't break the threads with your hands, but the threads are very delicate."

Ashly nodded and said, "Very, very delicate. When you are good to each other, new threads grow. When you help each other, new threads grow. The braid becomes thick and bright. But when you argue, threads break. When you are angry, threads break. When you do something mean, threads break. Then the braid gets thinner and thinner until there is no more braid. Sometimes, there may be only one thread left. If that last thread breaks, you cannot be married anymore.

Most people don't know about the threads of light because they can't see them. But we have a special wedding present for you. Here it is. When you look through these glasses, you can see the threads of light.

Lark looked through the glasses. Then Maya looked through the glasses. She saw many threads of light. Some threads sparkled in different colors. They were woven into a braid. She looked for a long time. When she took off the glasses, she said, "I did not believe it was possible. But I saw the threads of light with my own eyes. Thank you, Oaker. Thank you, Ashly. This is the most wonderful wedding present of all."

When Lark and Maya came home, they didn't know where to put the special glasses. In their bedroom, they had a table with a drawer where Maya kept important things. When she opened the drawer, Lark saw a bracelet. It was made of gold, like a large gold ring with designs all around it. Maya said, "This bracelet belonged to my grandmother. I don't wear it often because it is not good for a doctor to wear a bracelet while working in the hospital. But I keep it in this drawer so it will be safe. We can put the glasses here too."

2. The Threads of Light

At first, Lark and Maya opened the drawer every day to take out the glasses and look through them. They always saw the threads of light and the braid. The braid was always thick. It did not change. After some time, they looked through the glasses less often, maybe once a week. After more time, they looked through the glasses still less often, maybe once a month. They were no longer surprised when they looked through the glasses. They knew what to expect. They were sure the threads of light and the braid would be there. They did not think they needed to look through the glasses so often. They almost forgot that they had the glasses.

Lark and Mole were good friends. Sometimes Mole came to visit Lark and Maya. Sometimes Lark came to visit Mole in the store where Mole made shoes. When Lark came, Mole put aside his work. He got up from his workbench and talked with Lark. They talked about all things that happened in the town. They talked about other things too.

One day Lark came to visit Mole. Right away he saw something shiny on Mole's arm. He came closer and saw that it was Maya's bracelet. He thought to himself, "How can this be? How did Mole get this bracelet?" When Mole saw that Lark was looking at the bracelet, Mole smiled and said, "This bracelet means a lot to me." Lark did not say anything. He did not know what to think. "Perhaps," he thought to himself, "this is a different bracelet, a bracelet that looks just like Maya's bracelet." He went home and opened the drawer. The bracelet was gone.

Lark thought to himself, "Why did Maya give her bracelet to Mole? Perhaps Maya likes Mole more than she likes me." He felt bad. The longer he thought about it, the more bad he felt. Then he began to feel angry. He was angry at Mole and he was angry at Maya. The drawer of the desk was still open. The glasses were right in front of him. He looked through them. The braid was still there, but it was much thinner than before. Many threads of light were gone, and those that remained did not sparkle as much as before. Now Lark felt really bad. He thought that the braid was thin because Maya did not want to be married to him anymore.

When Maya came home, she asked Lark, "What's the matter, Lark?" Lark said, "Nothing." Maya asked, "Did something happen, Lark?" Lark said, "No." Maya said, "You look like you feel bad." Lark said, "I feel fine." Maya asked, "Did I do anything, Lark? Are you mad at me?" Lark said, "You didn't do anything. I'm not mad at you." Then they had dinner.

Lark and Maya usually talked while they had dinner. But they didn't talk this time. They ate their dinner without talking. Then Lark went into another room without saying anything.

The next day was Lark's birthday. When he came home, Maya said, "Happy birthday, Lark. I have baked a chocolate cake for your birthday." When Maya brought in the cake, Lark said, "The cake has whipped cream on it. I don't like whipped cream." Maya took the cake out of the room. After a while, she came back. She had taken the whipped cream off the cake. "Here it is," she said, "can I cut a piece for you?" Lark did not answer. Maya cut two pieces, a small one for herself and a big one for Lark. Lark took one bite and said, "The cake is not sweet enough," and he left the room. He opened the drawer and put on the glasses. The braid was gone. There was just one single thread of light. When Lark saw this thread, he became frightened. He was afraid the last thread would break. He was so afraid that he went right back into the other room. Maya was crying.

"Don't cry, Maya," he said, "please don't cry. I feel very bad. I am very ashamed, but I will tell you why I feel bad. Yesterday I went to Mole's store, and Mole had your bracelet. Mole is more handsome than I. I thought that maybe you have given your bracelet to Mole because you like Mole better than you like me."

When Lark said this, Maya stopped crying. She got up and gave Lark a big hug. She said, "Poor Lark, poor silly Lark, poor deer silly Lark. Don't you know that you are my everything?" Lark felt much better, but he said, "What happened to the bracelet?" And Maya said, "I promise I will tell you what happened, but not today. I will tell you tomorrow. Go see Mole tomorrow morning. Tell him you want to look at the words on the inside of the bracelet to make sure they are right. Read them. Then come home and I will tell to you what happened. OK?" And Lark nodded.

Early next morning, Lark went to Mole's store. As soon as Mole saw him, he got up. Lark said, "Can I look at the bracelet? I want to make sure the words are right." Mole took off the bracelet and gave it to Lark. The words engraved on the inside of the bracelet were: "To my best friend Mole, from Lark." Mole asked, "Are the words right?" And Lark said, "Oh yes, they are right. They are perfect." Then Mole said, "You have made me very happy, Lark. The mailman said he had a package for me. I could not think who would send me a package. Then I opened it and found it was from you. You sent me the most beautiful bracelet I have ever seen. When I read the words, I cried, because I always wanted you to be my friend. I was also happy that I got a present. I never got a present before. This is the first present I have ever gotten. I will always keep it. Thank you, Lark. Thank you." And Lark said, "I am very happy too, Mole."

When Lark came home, Maya said to him, "Now I will tell you what happened. I thought a lot about your birthday. I decided I would bake you a chocolate cake and would give you my grandmother's bracelet. Then I remembered that you often said that Mole is your best friend. You said that you wanted to give him a present, but you did not want to give him an ordinary present, the kind one buys in a store. You wanted to give him a special present to show him you are his friend. But you didn't know what to give him. So I decided I would not just give you the bracelet. I would give you an even better present. I would help you give a present to your friend Mole. I thought you would like this.

"I took the bracelet to the engraver. I wrote down the words he should put on the inside of the bracelet. He promised he would not send the bracelet to Mole until after your birthday. I wanted to tell you about the bracelet while we ate the chocolate cake. But the engraver made a mistake. He sent the bracelet to Mole too soon. So you saw it before I could tell you."

Lark said, "I behaved very badly, Maya. I am sorry. Please forgive me. You gave me a wonderful present."

"Now," Maya said, "I want you to promise me something. Promise me that if you ever feel bad, or if you are ever mad at me, you will tell me about it right away. Even if you don't want to tell, even if you are ashamed to tell, you will tell me right away. Do you promise?" Lark said, "I promise." And Maya said, "I promise you the same thing." Maya hugged Lark and Lark hugged Maya.

Then Lark said, "Could we have my birthday cake now?" Maya said, "We will have the cake and tea." Maya made herbal tea. She is a doctor and she believes herbal tea is better for you than regular tea. Again she cut a small piece of cake for herself and a big piece of cake for Lark. When Lark started to eat the cake, Maya asked, "Do you think the cake is not sweet enough?" And Lark said, "Don't be ridiculous. This is absolutely the very best cake I have ever eaten in my whole life. The only thing that would make it better is if it had whipped cream on it." And they both laughed.

Lark ate the entire piece of cake Maya had given him. He even ate the crumbs.

Then Lark went into the other room. The blinds were down and the curtains were closed. The room was dark. But Lark went to the drawer, and put on the glasses. The braid was thicker than it had ever been. There were many new threads of light. They sparkled in different colors. They shone brightly in the dark.

3. The Forgetting Chain

Stari worked in the office of the Fuller furniture company. She typed letters. Her fingers flew over the keyboard. She typed very fast. She was a very good typist. She never made mistakes. But Stari didn't have a good opinion of herself. She didn't think being able to type well was important. Stari never wore fancy clothes. Her hair was long in front. It covered her forehead, right down to her eyebrows. She thought all of her girlfriends were prettier than she.

Most of the girls in the office where Stari worked had boyfriends. Stari didn't have a boyfriend. When she came home from work, she fixed dinner for herself. She ate her dinner alone. Then she sat around doing nothing.

One day, Lily, one of the girls in Stari's office, told Stari about the skating rink. Lily said, "Why don't you come with me. Ice skating is a lot of fun." Stari said, "But I can't skate." Lily said, "You can take lessons and learn. There is a very handsome skating teacher at the rink. You can take lessons from him. You have to pay him one dollar for every lesson. He will teach you to skate." Stari said, "No. I don't think he can teach me. I think skating is beautiful, but lessons won't help. I will never be able to skate."

Lily said, "How do you know if you don't try?" Stari said, "I tried. When I was 5 years old, my mother took me to a skating rink. There was a skating teacher there. He told me what to do. I couldn't do it. The teacher said, 'You are stupid. You will never be able to skate.' When I was 10 years old, my mother said, 'All the other girls can skate. Why

13

can't you skate? What's the matter with you?' She took me to the skating rink again. There was another teacher there. My mother told the teacher, 'Stari can't skate. Perhaps she is stupid. Will you try to teach her?' The teacher said, 'I am a very good teacher. I have taught many people to skate.' Then the teacher showed me what to do. When I tried, he said, 'No, not like this. Do it like this.' In the end, he said, 'If I can't teach you, no one can teach you. You are stupid. You will never be able to skate.'"

Lily didn't want Stari to feel bad. She said, "Come with me to the skating rink. Talk to the teacher. His name is Glider. Ask him to give you lessons. If he says yes, get skating shoes that really fit. You don't have to skate now. Just come and see."

Next weekend, Stari went with Lily to the skating rink. Many people were there. Some of them could dance on the ice. Some could just skate forward and backward. Some could just go around, going forward all the time. But all could skate.

Then Stari saw Glider. When Glider skated, the people went to the sides and watched. Glider moved very fast. He made big circles on the ice. He jumped. He turned in the air. He looked like a bird flying. He was the most handsome man Stari had ever seen. Stari thought to herself, "If I take lessons from Glider, he will have to hold my arm." Stari wanted Glider to hold her arm. She asked him, "Can you teach me to skate?" Glider looked at her. He shrugged, and said, "You will have to pay me one dollar for each lesson."

Stari went to an ice skating store. She tried on many skating shoes. She didn't like any of them. Then she remembered Mole's store and went there. She said to Mole, "I can't skate. I've never been able to skate. But I want to take lessons. A friend told me that if I get good shoes, I will perhaps be able to skate. Can you make me good shoes?" Mole said, "I will make you shoes that fit perfectly. Buy blades that are perfectly sharp. I'll attach the perfect blades to the perfect shoes. Then you'll have perfect skates."

Stari picked up her skates. A few weeks later, she came back to Mole. She looked very sad. Mole asked, "What's the matter, Stari? Is anything wrong with your shoes?" Stari began to cry. She said, "It isn't the shoes. The shoes fit perfectly. It's me. I can't do anything right." Mole said, "You can type very fast. And you never make mistakes. Surely this is something you're doing right." Stari said, "Yes. But typing isn't important. I pay Glider for lessons. He takes my money and I learn nothing. He says I'm doing everything wrong. 'No, no, no,' he yells, 'Not this way. Do it like I show you.' Then he skates all around the rink to show off for the pretty girls. That's all he cares about, his skating and the pretty girls. I'm not pretty enough for Glider." Mole looked at her very carefully, and said, "It's true, Stari, that you are not pretty. You are beautiful. I can see this clearly. Glider can't see it because Glider sees only himself."

Stari was surprised. She said, "You're a good person, Mole. But you can't fool me. I know you're just saying this to make me feel good. But that's not why I came back. I came because a friend of mine said that she talked to a friend. That friend talked to another friend. That friend said she heard from someone that you know about magic. Do you think there's any magic that can help me?" Mole said, "I thought once that there is magic. Now I don't know. Go talk to two friends of mine, Lark and Maya. Lark is a poet. Every poet uses magic. That's part of being a poet. Maya is a doctor. She believes in science, not magic. But she's a good doctor. And a good doctor knows that there's much in the world we don't know and don't understand. Maybe they will be able to help you."

Stari thanked Mole and went to see Lark and Maya. She told them about the ice rink. She told them that she couldn't skate. She told them that she needed magic. Lark and Maya talked with each other. Then Maya said, "We have two friends, Oaker and Ashly. They are the wisest people we know. They live in a cabin half way up the mountain. We will visit them soon. If you want, you can come with us. You can talk with Oaker and Ashly. Maybe they'll have some magic for you."

Next weekend, Lark and Maya took Stari along. They hiked up to the cabin where Oaker and Ashly lived. When they got there, Maya said, "This is Stari. She wants to learn to skate. She tried to learn when she was 5 years old, but she couldn't. She tried to learn when she was 10 years old, but she couldn't. She tried to learn again now she is grown up, but she still can't."

Ashly said, "Ice skating is how Oaker and I met. Oaker is a very good skater. He won a medal for skating." Oaker laughed and said, "Ashly is a very good skater. She was my teacher. I took lessons from Ashly." Ashly laughed and said, "Oaker pretended that he couldn't skate, so he could hold on to me." And Oaker said, "Until Ashly used magic. Then I couldn't pretend any more. We became partners. And we married."

Stari asked, "What kind of magic did Ashly use?" Ashly said, "I'll show you." She left the room. After a while she came back. She carried a chain. It was made of silver, but it was almost completely black because it hadn't been polished for a long time. It wasn't a heavy chain. One could put it around one's neck and wear it like a necklace.

Ashly showed the chain to Stari and said, "This is a forgetting chain. This chain will help you. But tell me first, do you have a teacher?" Stari said, "Yes, I have a teacher. I pay him a dollar for every lesson, but he doesn't think I'll ever learn. He doesn't pay attention to me. He only likes pretty girls, and I am plain."

Oaker asked, "Who told you that you are plain?" Stari said, "My mother was very beautiful. She always said I was plain." Oaker said, "Don't you know that you are beautiful?" Stari said, "No, I never thought so. Mole said that I am beautiful, but I thought Mole only said this to make me feel good." Oaker said, "Mole makes shoes that fit perfectly. Anyone who can make anything perfect can see the truth. It doesn't matter what he makes. It can be a house, or a poem, or a pair of shoes. Such a person has better eyes than ordinary people. Such a person cannot be fooled by how things seem. Such a person sees how things really are."

Ashly asked, "Why do you keep your hair so it covers your forehead, Stari? Would you mind if I cut it for you?" Stari said, "I don't mind." Ashly took a pair of scissors. She cut all the hair away from Stari's forehead. She cut the back of Stari's hair just a little to make it round and fluffy. Then she gave Stari a mirror and asked, "Do you like it?" Stari said, "Thank you very much, Ashly. You are right. My hair looks better this way. But my hair isn't going to help me skate." Ashly said, "But the forgetting chain will help you."

Stari asked, "What is a forgetting chain?" Ashly said, "I will tell you in a moment. But first I want to ask you a few questions. Are there any other skating teachers at the rink?" Stari said, "Yes. There is Streamer." Ashly asked, "Can he skate well?" Stari said, "He doesn't skate often where people can see him. I think he is shy. I've never seen him talk to the pretty girls. But I saw him skate once. It was late in the evening. Most people had left already. He was the only one on the ice. He was as good as Glider. No. He was better than Glider." Ashly said, "Fine. From now on, take lessons only from Streamer. OK?" Stari said, "I will do anything you tell me, Ashly."

Ashly put the chain around Stari's neck and said, "Here is the forgetting chain. It's a present. You must always wear it when you skate. Will you promise me that?" Stari said, "Yes. I promise. But what does the forgetting chain do?" Ashly said, "The forgetting chain makes you forget that there are things you can't do. It is not a teacher. It won't make it possible for you to do anything you can't do. If you can't skate now, you still won't be able to skate when you wear the chain. But you'll forget that you can't skate. That's why it's called the forgetting chain."

The next time Stari went to the rink, she spoke to Streamer. He said he would give her lessons, but only late in the evening. He said this was because the ice was clear then. But Stari thought it was because he didn't want people to watch. When Stari came for her first lesson, Streamer asked, "What can you do on the ice?" Stari was wearing the forgetting chain. She said, "I don't know what I can do. Let's find out." Streamer said, "Just walk on the ice." Stari took one step and fell. She laughed, got up, and said, "I can do it." She took another step and fell again. She laughed again and said, "Don't worry, Streamer. I'm sure I can do it." She took another step. This time, she didn't fall. She took another step and another step. The ice was slippery and she started sliding forward. She got excited, and cried out, "I'm moving, Streamer. I'm moving. It's moving me along all by itself. It's wonderful." And she fell again. Streamer helped her up and said, "You are doing very well. It's good that you know you can do it." Stari laughed and said, "Why not? Of course I can do it. I may just have to practice for a while."

Stari came for lessons twice a week. Soon she could skate around the rink by herself. Streamer showed her how to skate backwards. That was a lot of fun. Streamer taught her to bend her knees, to keep her body straight, to use her arms, to turn, to stop, to make big circles. Stari always wore her forgetting chain. Whenever Streamer showed her a new thing, Stari said, "Yes, I see. I can do this." Stari fell many times. When she fell, she always laughed. She said to Streamer, "Just be patient, Streamer. I will do it again, and again, and again, until I do it right, because I know I can do it."

Streamer began to teach her more difficult moves, to spin, to lean backwards, to jump, to turn in the air. She learned to do all of them. Streamer was amazed. He said, "No one I know has ever learned so much so fast, Stari. It's almost like magic." Stari smiled, and said, "Who knows, Streamer. Perhaps it is magic."

Stari came to practice every evening, even when she didn't have a lesson. And Streamer began to teach Stari to dance on the ice. One day, he said, "I cannot be your teacher anymore. I cannot give you lessons anymore, because now you can skate as well as I. But if you want, you can be my skating partner. We can help each other. We can learn together. We can practice for the skating competition. And we can try to win a prize." Stari liked this very much.

One day, Glider saw Stari skate. He didn't recognize her, and said, "You skate very well. Do you want to be my skating partner?" And Stari said, "Thank you. I already have a skating partner." She was surprised that she had ever thought Glider was handsome. She did not think so now. She thought Streamer was much more handsome.

When Stari and Streamer talked together, which was every day, Streamer didn't say much. Stari talked more. But it didn't feel like only one person was talking, because Stari always knew what Streamer was thinking.

Stari and Streamer skated in the dance competition. The people liked the way Stari and Streamer skated. They clapped much more for them than for any of the other skaters. Stari and Streamer won first prize.

After the competition, Streamer said, "I want to talk to you about something, Stari." Stari waited. Streamer said nothing. Then he suddenly got up and said, "I forgot to turn off the lights in the locker room. Please wait for me. I'll be right back." He left. When he came back, Streamer didn't say anything. They just sat looking at each other. Then Streamer got up again and said, "I forgot to lock up my skates. Please wait for me. I'll be right back." When Streamer came back the second time, Stari said, "Hold still for a moment. I just want to see how this chain looks on you." She took off the chain, and before Streamer knew what was happening, she put it around his neck." She looked at him, and said, "It looks very nice."

Streamer said, "Stari I like you more than I like anyone else in the whole world." Stari said, "Yes." Streamer said, "I want us to be partners, always." Stari said, "Yes." Streamer said, "I want us to be partners not only for skating. I want us to be partners for all things. I want us to be married." Stari said, "Yes." Streamer said, "You want it too?" Stari said, "Of course." Streamer gave Stari a big hug. Stari gave Streamer a big hug. Then she said, "My chain looks very good on you. But now I need it back." He took the chain off and put it around her neck.

Stari and Streamer were married by a double-judge, right on the skating rink. They called the judge a double-judge, because he was a judge in the court, but he was also a judge in the skating competition. It was a small wedding. They invited only a few people, Lark and Maya, Mole, Streamer's sister, Stari's friend Lily, and of course, Oaker and Ashly.

After the wedding, they all sat around a large table, talking. Streamer said, "I've always wondered about Stari's chain. Stari never took it off, except once. And then only for a very short time. Is there anything special about this chain?" Ashly said, "It's a forgetting chain." Lark said, "It's magic." Oaker said, "It makes you forget that you can't do something that maybe you can do." Streamer said, "Really? Does it work for all people?" Ashly said, "Yes, but only when they need it." Streamer asked, "Would it work for me?" Ashly said, "Of course. But only if there was something you wanted to do, but thought you couldn't do." Streamer said, "I have a very smart wife."

Stari asked, "Do I have to wear the chain always?" Ashly answered, "No. I meant to tell you. You can take it off now. You don't need to wear it any more." Streamer kept staring at the chain. Stari asked, "What should I do with it?" Ashly said, "Keep it safely. Someday you'll meet someone who needs it. Then you'll give it to that person. It will help that person just as it has helped you. Someday, that person will give it to someone else. So the forgetting chain will be passed on from one person to another. It will help many people, because most of us don't know what we can do, and there's only one way to find out. Isn't that right, Stari?" And Stari said, "Yes, that's right. We must be willing to fall, and fall, and fall, many times just to find out what we can do."

Streamer leaned forward and looked at Ashly. His voice trembled when he asked, "Tell me, Ashly. Was it really magic? I mean real, real magic?" Maya answered for Ashly, "It worked, didn't it? So it must have been magic." Ashly smiled.

4. The Silver Mirror

Glider and Streamer were very good skaters. They could jump, spin, and dance on ice. They were both skating teachers at the rink. Streamer was married. He was married to his skating partner, Stari. He was very happy. Glider was not married. He had a girlfriend. Whenever a new pretty girl came to the rink, Glider broke up with his girlfriend. Then the new girl became his girlfriend.

One day, Glider and Streamer left the rink at the same time. They did not usually talk much. They weren't really friends. They said hello and goodbye. They didn't talk about important things. Now they were walking side by side. Streamer didn't know what to say, so he said, "I saw you skating today." Glider asked, "Did I look good? Did you see my triple jump? Did you like my new skating outfit?" Streamer said, "Your jump was very good. Your skating outfit is very nice." Glider said, "Blue is a very good color for me. My new girlfriend, Azalea, says I'm the most handsome man she has ever known. Do you know Azalea? She is new at the rink." Streamer said, "I've seen her." Glider said, "She's very pretty. Don't you think?" Streamer said, "Yes, she's very pretty." Glider said, "When I have the same girlfriend too long, I get bored. But all the girls like me. I can always get a new girlfriend."

Streamer asked, "Are you ever sad?" Glider said, "I? No. I'm never sad. I'm the best skater in town. I'm very handsome. All the girls like me. Why should I be sad?" Streamer said, "Sometimes, people who say they have everything are sad. Besides, there's a germ that makes people sad." Glider said, "A germ? Really? What kind of a germ? What else does it do besides making you sad?" Streamer said, "I don't believe it does anything else. A person with this germ has no fever. He remains strong. But if he gets no medicine, he gets sadder and sadder all the time." Glider asked, "You mean there is a medicine you can take for this germ?" Streamer said, "I think so." Glider said, "This is hard to believe. Who told you so?" Streamer said, "A doctor at the hospital told me. Her name is Maya. She's a very good doctor." Just then they came to the place where Streamer had to go in a different direction. They said good-bye, and Glider went on by himself.

There was a beggar on the next corner. The beggar said, "Please, sir, give me some money. I am hungry." Glider said, "If you are hungry, get a job." The beggar said, "I have tried to get a job. But my left arm just hangs there. I can't move it. No one wants to give me a job." Glider said, "Get a job where you don't have to move your left arm." And he walked on.

The skating rink was open on Saturdays and Sundays because many people wanted to skate on the weekend. It was closed on Wednesdays. Glider had a lot of time on Wednesday. His girlfriend, Azalea, was at her job. Glider walked around for a while. Then he went to the hospital, and asked to see Maya.

Maya asked, "Why have you come? Are you sick? Do you have any pain?" Glider said, "I don't have any pain, and I'm not sick. I have everything. I'm very handsome, but you can see this for yourself. I'm the best skater in town. All the girls like me. But I hear there's a germ that makes people sad. And I came to find out about this germ." Maya said, "I see. Well, let me examine you." She took a light and looked into Glider's eyes, and said, "Your eyes are fine." She asked Glider to open his mouth wide, and said, "Your throat is fine." She asked Glider to take off his shirt and take a deep breath. She listened while he breathed, and said, "Your lungs are fine." She put a stethoscope on his chest. This is a little cup with two long tubes doctors use to listen to the beating of the heart. She listened once. Then she listened again. Then she listened a third time. She said something to herself that Glider couldn't hear. Glider asked, "Is anything wrong? Is anything wrong with my heart?"

Maya said, "Put your shirt on. Then we'll talk." Glider put on his shirt and asked, "What's the matter with my heart?" Maya said, "Don't be afraid." Glider said, "I'm not afraid. I'm very brave. What about my heart? Is something wrong with my heart?" Maya said, "You are just fine. Your heart is strong, but you have a strange heart beat. That's all." Glider asked, "And what about the germ that makes people sad. Do I have this germ?" Maya said, "I have never heard of a germ that makes people sad. Where did you get this idea?" Glider said, "Streamer said you told him about such a germ." Maya said, "I know Streamer. He is very nice. I know his wife, Stari. She is very nice too. I was at their wedding. I talked with Streamer about germs. Maybe I said something that gave him this idea. But I don't know of any germ that makes people sad. Now, about your heart."

Glider said, "You said my heart is fine." Maya said, "Your heart is fine. You have a strong heart. But you have a strange heart beat, a one-five heart beat. First, there's one extra-strong beat. Then, there are five regular beats. Your heart keeps on beating this way, steady and regular, like a clock. One-five, one-five, one-five. I never heard about this kind of beat when I studied to become a doctor. But a man I know told me that he once had a one-five beat when he was young. He said that, at that time, he was often very sad."

Glider said, "But I'm not sad." Maya continued, "I'm not saying you are sad. I'm just telling you what the man told me. He told me that after the beat changed, he was not sad anymore. I don't know what he did to change his beat. But I know that a one-five beat is nothing to worry about. The man who had it is now very old and very strong and very healthy. He's a skater like you. When he was young, he won a prize for skating. His name is Oaker. He lives in a cabin half way up the mountain. You can go up and visit him and find out what happened to him." Glider said, "Maybe I don't want to go half way up the mountain. Old people are not much fun. All they want to talk about is sicknesses." Maya said, "That's all right. You don't have to go. I'm only a doctor. There's nothing wrong with you that I can cure. Goodbye."

When Glider walked back from the hospital, he passed the beggar on the street corner. The beggar said, "Won't you help me, please?" Glider shook his head, and said, "No, I won't. Other people give you money. But I don't believe in giving money to beggars. If no one gave money to beggars, the beggars would stop begging." The beggar said, "Perhaps they would starve and die." Glider said, "I'm willing to wait and see." And he walked on.

On Wednesday, Glider went up the mountain early in the morning. He came to the clearing where Oaker and Ashly's cabin was. Oaker came out. Glider said to him, "I'm looking for an old man. He lives somewhere here. His name is Oaker. Do you know where I can find him?" Oaker said, "I am Oaker." Glider said, "I thought Oaker is an old man." Oaker said, "I am an old man. Did you come for any special purpose?" Glider said, "I went to see a doctor in the hospital. Her name is Maya. She said I have a one-five heart beat. I'm a skater. I'm the best skater in town. She said you were a skater once." Oaker said, "I am still a skater." Glider said, "She told me you had a one-five heart beat once. She said that maybe you could help me." Oaker asked, "Are you sad?" Glider didn't answer. Instead, he asked, "What did you do to change your heart beat?" Oaker said, "I will tell you, but let's have lunch first."

They went inside the cabin. Ashly was there. Oaker said, "Ashly, this is Glider. He tells me he's the best skater in town." Ashly smiled and said, "That happens." Glider didn't know what to think. Ashly continued, "I can see that Glider is very handsome. I bet he gives skating lessons. I bet he has many girlfriends. I bet all his girlfriends are very pretty." Oaker said, "He has come because he has a one-five heart beat." Ashly turned to Glider and said, "Really? This is very interesting. Are you sad?" Glider said, "Why is everyone asking me if I'm sad? I don't have any reason to be sad. I'm handsome. I'm the best skater in town. I have a new girlfriend, Azalea. She's the prettiest girl in town." Ashly said, "That's wonderful." Glider said, "I'm not sad. Not really sad. Not sad enough to worry about." And Ashly said, "I have fresh bread and cheese for lunch, and blueberry pie. Do you like that?" Glider said, "Yes, Ashly. Thank you. I like that very much."

After lunch, Oaker put his arm around Glider and led him out of the cabin. They went to the edge of the clearing. They could see the town below. They could see the mountains in the distance. Oaker took something out of a pocket and said, "This is a silver mirror. Many years ago, it helped me change. Perhaps it will help you too." He gave the mirror to Glider. The mirror was a thin round disk that could fit into the palm of a hand. Glider could hold it in his palm and look into it. It was the brightest and shiniest mirror Glider had ever seen.

Oaker said, "Look into the mirror and tell me what you see." Glider said, "It's a mirror, isn't it? What's there to see?" Oaker said, "Just look and tell me what you see." Glider said, "I see myself. It's a very good mirror. It reflects very well. I'm very handsome." Oaker said, "All right. This mirror is a present. You can keep it. When you get to town, visit Maya. Ask her to look into the mirror and tell you exactly what she sees. Then ask Lark, that's Maya's husband, to tell you exactly what he sees. Then ask Mole, the shoemaker, to tell you exactly what he sees. Then come back and we'll talk." Glider said, "It's just a mirror. What's the point of asking all those people what they see?" Oaker said, "I'll explain it to you when you come back." Glider said, "Why can't you explain it to me right now. It would save me a trip. It's a long climb to get up here. Perhaps I won't come back." Oaker said, "That's up to you. You don't have to come back. The silver mirror is yours. You can do anything you want with it.

But if you do exactly what I told you to do, maybe it'll help you change the one-five heart beat. And one more thing. You say you're not sad. But if you were sad, maybe it would also help you not be sad anymore."

Glider went back to the town. It was evening by the time he got there. He went directly to Lark and Maya's house. Maya was surprised to see him. He asked her to tell him exactly what she saw in the silver mirror. She looked and said, "I see a room in the hospital. There are four beds. There's a patient in each bed, a woman with pneumonia, a man waiting for a heart operation, a little girl with high fever, and a little boy with a broken leg." Glider was surprised. He took a quick look in the mirror. But it was still just an ordinary mirror. He saw himself. Maya asked Lark to come in from the other room. Lark looked into the mirror, and said, "I see a desk. There's paper on the desk. A pen is writing on the paper. The pen is writing all by itself. It is writing very fast." Next morning, Glider went to Mole's store. He asked Mole to look into the mirror. Mole said, "I see three pairs of shoes, a pair of slippers, a pair of walking shoes, and a pair of boots. They are made of the best leather. They will fit perfectly."

Glider went back up the mountain. Oaker was happy to see him. He wanted to know whether Maya, Lark and Mole had told Glider what they saw in the mirror. Glider said, "Yes, they told me. But what kind of mirror is this anyway?" Oaker said, "It's a silver mirror. It shows everyone what is in their hearts. It shows them what they really care about. If there is nothing they care about, they see only themselves. If they don't even care about themselves, the mirror turns blank. Maya cares about sick people. Lark cares about writing poems. Mole cares about making shoes. You don't care about anything. That's why you see only yourself. That's why you have a one-five heart beat. One extra-strong beat for yourself. The regular beats for everything else. That's why you are sad."

Glider said, "All people care about themselves. Lark stands on the platform. He wants people to like his poems. He wants people to tell him he's a good poet." Oaker said, "Yes, but he also wants to write good poems. One can care about oneself. But one must also have something else to care about." Glider said, "I care about skating, don't I?" Oaker said, "Maybe you cared about skating when you started. But you stopped learning, and you got bored. Now you don't care about skating anymore." Glider said, "This is ridiculous. Take back your mirror. I don't want it."

Oaker said, "Many years ago, I had a one-five heart beat, just like you. I was sad and mean all the time. Then a wise woman gave me this mirror. The mirror helped me change." Glider said, "Maybe I don't want to change. Maybe I like myself just the way I am. Maybe I will just throw the mirror away." Oaker said, "That's up to you. I have given it to you. Now it is yours. Maybe it will help you. Maybe it won't. You can keep it. You can throw it away. You can give it away. You can sell it. You can do anything you want with it."

Glider thought about the mirror while he was walking back to town. It was a long walk. So he thought about the mirror for a long time. He was angry at Oaker. He thought, "Oaker is just a silly old man. The mirror is just a trick. I don't have to pay attention to it." But these thoughts did not help him. He felt very bad. Then he said to himself, "I will test the mirror. I will give money to the beggar, and I will see whether anything changes in the mirror."

The next time Glider passed the beggar, he gave him a coin. The beggar said, "I am glad you have changed. Thank you. God bless you." But nothing changed in the mirror. Glider saw only himself. Then Glider thought, "One time may not be enough to make a difference. I'll give the beggar money every time I pass him next month. And I won't look into the mirror until the month is over."

From that time on, Glider gave the beggar money every time he saw him. The beggar always said, "Thank you. God bless you." This made Glider feel good. He thought to himself, "I help this beggar. I always give him money. I'm a very good person." After a full month had passed, Glider looked into the mirror. Nothing had changed. He saw himself, just as before. Then he looked more closely, and saw that something had changed. He still wore the same blue skating outfit he had always worn in the mirror, but now there was a gold medal on his chest. It was not the kind of medal they hang around your neck when you win a skating competition. It was the kind of medal soldiers get. It was pinned to the shirt.

Seeing the medal made Glider feel bad. He said to himself, "I don't like this mirror. I'm not going to look into it anymore. There is a silver store in the center of the town. The next time I pass by that store, I will sell the mirror. I'm sure they'll give me a lot of money for it." Glider put the mirror into a zipper pocket on the inside of his jacket. But he didn't go to the center of the town. He didn't pass the silver store. He forgot that he had wanted to sell the mirror. He forgot that he had put it into the inside pocket of his jacket. He forgot that he even had the mirror. But he continued to give money to the beggar every time he saw him. It had become a habit. Glider thought, "It doesn't matter why I give him money. Perhaps I do it only so I can pretend I am a good person. But it makes me feel good. So I do it."

One day, Glider saw a boy he had never seen before at the skating rink. It was a young boy, perhaps 12 years old. Glider saw the way the boy held his head, the way he held his arms. The boy could not do everything he tried to do, but every move he made was beautiful. When Glider was sitting on a bench, the boy sat down next to him. Glider asked, "What's your name?" The boy said, "Flyer." Glider asked, "How long have you been skating?" Flyer said, "Three months." Glider asked, "Who is your teacher?" Flyer said, "I have no teacher." Glider asked, "How did you learn to skate?" Flyer said, "I watched the good skaters. I tried to do what they do. I also tried to figure out for myself how things should be done." Glider said, "I'm a skating teacher. If you want, I'll give you lessons." Flyer said, "I would like this very much, but I have no money." Glider thought for a moment. Then he said, "You don't have to pay me. I'll give you free lessons." Flyer said, "That's wonderful. Thank you very much."

Glider began to give Flyer lessons. At first, it was two lessons a week. Then it was three. Then it was a lesson every day. Glider's girlfriend, Azalea, was surprised. She asked, "Why do you give Flyer free lessons?" Glider said, "Because he doesn't have the money to pay me." Azalea said, "That's not what I meant. Why do you give him lessons at all when he can't pay you?" Glider said, "Flyer will be a wonderful skater someday. He will fly like a bird." Azalea asked, "You mean, he will be a better skater than you?" Glider said, "Oh yes. Much better. Much much better. I'm a good skater, but even Streamer is a better skater than I." Azalea said, "Oh no, Glider. You are the best skater that ever was." Glider said, "Streamer is better than I. For a long time I didn't want to admit it. I can admit it now, but it isn't important. I doesn't matter which of us, Streamer or I, can skate better. What matters is Flyer."

Azalea was surprised. She said, "I don't understand you, Glider. Why does Flyer matter?" Glider said, "Because Flyer will not just be the best skater in town. He will not just be the best skater in the country. Someday Flyer will be the best skater in the world." Azalea said, "You want him to get a medal, so he'll get a lot of money, and will be able to pay you for the lessons?" Glider said, "I don't care whether he gets a medal. I don't care whether he gets money. I don't care whether he'll ever pay me. Someday, Flyer's skating will be the most beautiful skating in the world. When that time comes, I want to be able to watch him skate." Azalea said, "I always knew skaters are crazy. But you are the craziest of them all." And she gave him a hug.

When Glider saw the beggar on the street, Glider always gave him money. One day, Glider didn't have any money. While he was looking for money in his pockets, he felt something hard. He remembered the silver mirror. He didn't want to disappoint the beggar. He opened the zipper of the inside pocket of his jacket. He gave the mirror to the beggar, and said, "I have no money today. But this mirror is made of silver. Take it to the silver store in the middle of the town. They will buy it from you." The beggar took the mirror. As always, he said, "Thank you very much. God bless you."

Two days later, Glider was walking on the other side of the street. The beggar saw him, and came running across the street. He reached Glider and said, "I've been looking for you. I have something that belongs to you." And he handed the silver mirror to Glider. Glider said, "But I gave it to you. What happened?" The beggar said, "I did like you told me. I went to the silver store. I asked the lady whether she wanted to buy the silver mirror. She wanted to give me a lot of money for it. I took it back and looked into it. I was surprised. I didn't see myself at all." Glider asked, "What did you see?" The beggar said, "I have a little boy. When I looked into the mirror, I saw my little boy. Then I knew this is not an ordinary mirror. It is a magic mirror. I could not just sell it. I thought perhaps you made a mistake. Perhaps you didn't know it was a magic mirror. I was hoping to see you. I wanted to give it back to you."

Glider said, "I cannot take it back. I gave it to you. It belongs to you now. But if you will sell it to me, I will buy it from you. I don't know how much money I have in my pockets. It may be a little or it may be a lot. If you are willing, I will buy it from you for the money I have in my pockets." The beggar said, "You don't have to buy it. It belongs to you." Glider said, "I want to buy it." The beggar said, "All right." Glider looked through his pockets. He gave the beggar all the money that was there. The beggar said, "You don't have to give me all this money. It's too much." Glider said, "That was the deal. And I want you to forgive me." The beggar said, "What for? There's nothing to forgive." Glider said, "I behaved badly. I said mean things to you." The beggar said, "It was a long time ago. I don't remember." Glider said, "I thought bad thoughts about you. Please forgive me." The beggar said, "You're a very strange man. Every time you pass me, you give me money. Now you give me a lot of money. And you want me to forgive you." Glider said, "Yes." The beggar said, "All right. I forgive you. I forgive you for every bad thing you think you have done. God bless you." Glider hugged the beggar. The beggar cried.

When Glider came home, he took out the mirror and looked into it. He did not see himself in the mirror. He saw an eagle. Its wings were spread wide apart. It was soaring high over the mountains.

5. The Count-Down Watch

One Sunday, a large traveling market came to town. The market had many stalls. A stall is just a store in a tent. The tent is open on one side. It can be set up in the morning and taken down in the evening. One can buy things there, just like in a regular store. One can buy clothes to wear, books to read, pictures to look at, things to eat, toys to play with, and other things. There was a stall for ladies dresses, a stall for blue jeans, a stall for hats, a stall for scarves. There was a stall for breads. There was a stall for nuts. There was a stall for chocolates. And there were other stalls of all kinds.

Many people came to the market. Some people came to buy things. Some people came to walk around and look. It was very exciting to walk around in the market because there were so many things to see.

Lark and Maya came to the market. They didn't come to buy any particular thing. They just wanted to see what was there. Maya liked to look at lady's clothes. Even if she didn't buy any, she liked to look at them. Lark didn't like to spend much time looking at lady's clothes. He always wanted to see what was in the next stall, and in the next one, and in the next one. So he wandered off by himself. He didn't spend much time at any stall. He looked and walked on. He knew that Maya was having a good time looking at lady's clothes. He wanted her to be happy. He knew he could turn back and find her quickly when he was finished looking.

When Lark passed one of the stalls, a man spoke to him. The man said, "Three balls for a dollar." The man wore strange clothes, a dark blue shirt with many white stars on it, big baggy purple pants, and a hat with a gigantic feather. Lark immediately called him Featherman in his mind. From the way Featherman spoke, Lark could tell that Featherman was from some far-away place where people speak a different language. Featherman pointed to his stall and said again, "Three balls for a dollar."

Lark looked into the stall. There was a long wooden shelf in the back of the stall. On this shelf, there were three empty soda cans. Stuffed animals hung from the side of the tent, teddy bears, lions, giraffes, monkeys. On the other side, there was a glass case with rings in it.

Featherman said, "You can win a prize. You throw the balls at the cans. If you hit a can, you get a prize." Lark said, "I'm not good at throwing a ball. Even when I was small, my friend Mole always threw a ball better than I." Featherman said, "It doesn't matter how you threw a ball when you were small. You can probably throw a ball much better now. Three balls for a dollar. If you hit one can, you get a stuffed animal. Any stuffed animal you want. You can pick it out. If you hit two cans, you get a ring. Any ring you want. You can pick it out. If you hit all three cans, you get a watch. This is your chance to get a prize." Lark said, "Maybe I don't want a prize." Featherman said, "No. That's not how it is. Some people say they don't want a prize, but in the end, everyone wants a prize."

Lark didn't like the way Featherman talked to him. He wanted to go on. But Featherman came out and stood right in his way. He stretched out his arm and held three balls right in front of Lark, and said again, "Three balls for a dollar." Lark didn't know what to do, so he said, "All right." He gave Featherman a dollar and took the three balls.

When Lark threw the first ball, he didn't try very hard. He just threw the ball in the direction of the cans. The ball hit a can. Lark was surprised. He threw the second ball. This ball too hit a can. Lark thought to himself, "I'm doing real well. I throw much better now than when I was small." He took careful aim with the third ball. The ball went far to the left. Lark was sure he had missed. But as the ball traveled through the air, it curved around and hit the third can.

Featherman said, "Very good. You win a prize. Here it is. A countdown watch. There are not many of them in the world. Take good care of it."

Lark took the watch. It was not the kind of watch you wear on your wrist. It was a bigger watch, an old-fashioned watch, a watch one carries in one's pocket. Lark said good-bye to Featherman and left. Now he was in a hurry. He wanted to find Maya and tell her that he had won a prize.

Lark ran back the way he had come. Soon he saw Maya. She was standing in front of a stall, looking at scarves. When he reached her, she said, "Look, isn't this a beautiful scarf?" But Lark didn't look at the scarf. He was too excited. "Guess what, Maya," he called out, "I won a prize." Maya asked, "How did you win a prize?" Lark said, "I hit three cans." Maya asked, "What is the prize?" Lark said, "A count-down watch." Then he stopped and asked, "Tell me, Maya. What is a count-down watch?" Maya looked at the watch and said, "I don't know."

Maya was a doctor. She knew many things. Lark was surprised that she didn't know what a count-down watch was. Maya asked, "Didn't you ask the man who gave you the prize?" Lark said, "No. I forgot to ask." Maya said, "Then let's go back and ask him now."

They started to walk back, but they didn't see the stall. Lark said, "It was somewhere near here." They walked past many stalls. Lark said, "It wasn't this far. I didn't see these stalls before. We must have walked right by it." They walked back and forth three times. They didn't see the stall. Maya said, "Perhaps the man was finished for the day and packed up his things and left?" Lark said, "There wasn't enough time for him to do this. And I don't see an empty space where his stall was." They asked people at other stalls, "Do you know a stall where one throws balls to win a prize?" No one knew.

Mole came walking toward them. Mole was Lark's best friend. He was a shoemaker. He made shoes that fit perfectly. Lark told Mole what had happened. Mole said, "I've been walking here since the market opened. I'm sure I have seen every stall. I'm sure I passed every stall two or three or four times. But I don't remember any stall where one could win a prize by hitting three cans. Perhaps you imagined it?" Lark shook his head, and said, "Did I imagine this?" He stretched out his hand and gave the watch to Mole. It was solid and heavy. Then Mole said, "If you can't find the man who gave you this watch, you must ask someone else. Why don't you go and ask the watchmaker. There is a sign in the window of his store that says 'We can repair any watch.' Surely he'll know what kind of a watch this is."

Lark and Maya went to the watchmaker. Lark asked, "Do you know what a count-down watch is?" The watchmaker said, "I have never heard of a count-down watch. But if you have one, let me see it." Lark gave him the watch. The watchmaker looked at the watch and said, "This is a very strange watch. It has an hour hand, and a minute hand, and a second-hand. These hands are moving. They show the exact time. The watch also has a space for numbers. You know, some watches don't have moving hands. They have a space where numbers show the time. This watch has such a space. The space is empty. There are no numbers. But the really strange thing is that I can't see what makes this watch run. There's no knob for winding it, or for setting the right time. If it runs on a battery, there must be a way to change the battery. But the watch is made of one piece all around. There's no crack anywhere for opening the watch. I've never seen a watch like this. I'm afraid I cannot help you."

Lark and Maya decided to visit Oaker and Ashly, the two people who had helped them get married. They lived in a cabin half way up the side of a mountain. Oaker and Ashly were very old and wise. They knew many things. Perhaps they would know about the count-down watch.

Next Saturday, Lark and Maya got up early in the morning. They put on the hiking shoes Mole had made for them. They took their backpacks, and they hiked to the clearing on the side of the mountain where Oaker and Ashly's cabin was. Oaker was chopping wood when they got there. He was happy to see them. He hugged Lark and he hugged Maya, and he asked, "How are the two of you getting along?" Lark and Maya both answered, "We are very happy." Then they laughed because they had said the same words at the same time.

Lark asked Oaker, "Do you know what a count-down watch is?" Oaker was silent for a moment. Then he asked, "Why do you want to know?" Lark said, "I want to know because I have a count-down watch." Oaker said slowly, "I have heard of a count-down watch. I have never seen one myself. But I knew someone once who had one." Lark was excited. He asked, "How does it work? What does it do?" Oaker was silent for a long time. Finally he said, "With a real count-down watch, you can tell when things will happen in the future. You can ask any question and the watch begins the count-down. Let me see it." Oaker looked at the watch from all sides. Then he said, "We must test it to see whether it is a real count-down watch. Come over here."

They walked to the edge of the clearing. From there one could see over the trees into the distance. The town looked tiny far below. Oaker said, "There are eagles up here. Every once in a while, an eagle flies by. Hold the watch to your lips and ask when you will next see an eagle flying by." Lark held the watch to his lips and asked, "When will I next see an eagle flying by?" They all looked at the watch. The number 3:34 had appeared in the space on the watch. The number was changing all the time. Oaker explained, "The watch showed that you will see an eagle 3 minutes and 34 seconds after you asked the question. By now it is 2 minutes and 15 seconds. The watch is counting backwards. It's counting the time remaining. That's why it's called a count-down watch. By now it's down to 55 seconds." The watch continued to count backwards. It reached 5 seconds, then 4, 3, 2, 1, 0. Just when it reached zero, an eagle flew by. Oaker said, "Yes. I believe you have a real count-down watch."

Ashly came out of the cabin. She was happy to see them. She hugged Maya. She hugged Lark. And she said, "You have come at the right time. I have baked bread, and I have baked a cake. We will have a good lunch."

Oaker looked at Ashly and said, "Lark has a count-down watch." Lark was excited. He said, "It really works. We just tested it. Isn't that wonderful?" Ashly didn't answer right away. Then she said, "Perhaps." Lark was surprised and said, "Why do you say perhaps? It really works. We saw it. All of us. Do you know what I can do with this watch? There are so many questions I can ask." Ashly said, "Yes, I know. I'm sure it works. What I meant was, perhaps this is wonderful."

Maya said, "Oaker and Ashly don't think that having a count-down watch is as wonderful as it seems."

Lark looked at Ashly. He looked at Oaker. He looked at Maya. No one said anything. Then Oaker began to speak, "A count-down watch can be a good thing. Or it can be a bad thing. It depends on who has it, and on what kind of questions they ask. I have known only one person who had one. It was someone I loved. It did not help that person." Lark asked, "But isn't it good to know things? Aren't we supposed to learn as much as we can?" Oaker answered, "Yes, it's good to know things. But knowing about the world is one thing and knowing the future is another. It's like reading the end of a book first. When you do that, you'll no longer have as much fun reading the book because you'll know how it turns out. And if you use a count-down watch, you'll no longer have as much fun in life, because you'll know how it turns out."

Ashly said, "There's one more thing. If you use a count-down watch, you'll no longer try to do your best. You'll ask the watch whether you'll succeed. The watch will tell you that you won't succeed, because the watch will know that after it has told you this, you won't try anymore. So you really won't succeed, and it will all come true." Oaker said, "It amounts to this: A count-down watch is good only if one can be wise enough to know exactly what to ask and what not to ask."

Lark thought about it for a while. Then he said, "All right, I can find out." He put the watch to his lips and asked, "When will I be wise enough to ask only questions that will help me and other people?" All four of them looked at the watch. There were no numbers in the space, only one word "Never." When she saw this, Maya took the watch out of Lark's hand, and before anyone knew what she was doing, she threw the watch with all her strength into the open space before them. They all thought the watch would fall down into the trees below. But the watch didn't fall down. It traveled straight out in the direction Maya had thrown it. They could see it moving further and further away. It became smaller and smaller and finally disappeared in the distance.

Lark said to Maya, "You are a good wife, Maya. Thank you." They hugged and went in to have lunch.

6. The Third Hill

Glider was a teacher at the ice skating rink. Azalea was his girl-friend. Azalea was a pretty girl. Azalea was very interested in clothes. She had many dresses. Most of her dresses were red. She also had a few dresses that weren't red. They were purple. She also had one bright blue dress.

Azalea always wore shoes with high heels. Her hair was always fluffy. And she always wore makeup. She spent half an hour every morning putting on her makeup. She had many different lipsticks. She put on one lipstick. Then she put on another lipstick on top of it. This made her lips sparkle. She put on eye makeup to make her eyelashes longer. She put on creams to make her skin smooth. She put on rouge to make her cheeks pink. When she came to the rink to meet Glider, Glider said, "You look wonderful." And Azalea said, "My dress is wrinkled. I'm a mess."

Azalea had ice skates, but she couldn't skate very well. She went around the rink twice. Then she said, "I have to take off these skating shoes. How can people keep them on for so long? They hurt my ankles." Then she took off her skates. But she liked to watch Glider skate. She said, "You are the best skater that ever was." Glider laughed.

Azalea liked to dance. She liked to dance more than she liked to do anything else. She wanted to go to the nightclub all the time. A night-club is a place where one can get things to eat and drink, and listen to music. When the musicians begin to play, people get up to dance. Most people do not dance to every song. They want to rest some of the time. Azalea never wanted to rest. She wanted to dance all the time. The only time she wanted to sit at the table was when the musicians took a rest.

Then she said, "Why do they rest so long? It's about time they started to play again."

Before Azalea became his girlfriend, Glider never danced. He was skating during the day. He didn't want to go dancing in the evening. But when he saw how much Azalea wanted to dance, he went to the nightclub with her.

In the beginning, Glider was not a very good dancer. You might think that anyone who can dance on ice, can dance on the dance floor. This is not so. Dancing on a dance floor and dancing on ice are different. But Glider learned fast. He didn't become a very, very good dancer, but good enough to dance with Azalea. After a while, he began to like dancing. He liked it because it made Azalea happy. When Azalea danced, she didn't think about her hair, or whether her dress was wrinkled, or whether her makeup was smudged. She thought only about dancing.

Glider was giving skating lessons to a boy. The boy's name was Flyer. He was 12 years old. Glider gave Flyer a lesson every day. He watched every move Flyer made. When Glider looked at Flyer, he saw not only what Flyer could do now, while he was still young. Glider also saw what Flyer would be able to do when he grew up. Glider believed that someday Flyer would look like a bird flying across the ice. He believed that someday Flyer would be the best skater in the world.

One day, Glider was trying to teach Flyer to do a forward leap. He told Flyer what to do. He showed him how to do it. Flyer didn't understand. Glider skated over to Streamer who was at the other end of the rink. Streamer was another skating teacher. Streamer was a very good skater. He and his partner, Stari, had won first prize in the ice dancing competition.

Glider said, "Streamer, would you do me a favor?" Streamer said, "I'll try. What is it?" Glider said, "I have been trying to show Flyer how to do a forward leap. I have explained it to him. I have shown it to him. He still can't do it. Would you mind doing it for us once or twice. Flyer and I will watch it together. I will point out to him what you are doing. Perhaps this will help him." Streamer said, "I'll be glad to do it." Streamer did the forward leap. Glider explained to Flyer what Streamer was doing. Then Flyer said, "Now I understand." Flyer did it himself. Everybody was happy.

Glider and Streamer had never talked much. Now they started talking. Streamer had never liked Glider. Now he started to like him. They became friends.

Streamer was married to Stari. She was also his skating partner. One day, Streamer said to Stari, "Could we invite Glider and his girlfriend to dinner?" Stari said, "I don't like Glider. He was very mean to me when he was giving me skating lessons. And I don't like Azalea." Streamer said, "But you don't know her. You've never even talked to her." Stari said, "She is one of those pretty girls. She always wears a red dress. She always wears makeup. I've never liked those pretty girls." Streamer said, "All right, we don't have to invite them."

Next day, Stari and Streamer were walking to the skating rink. They met Mole. They stopped and talked for a while. Stari asked Mole about Glider and Azalea. Mole said, "Be careful, Stari. There was a time when you couldn't skate. Then you got a magic chain. There are all kinds of magic in the world. Things aren't always what they seem. People aren't always what they seem." When they went on, Stari said to Streamer, "Go ahead and invite them."

Glider and Azalea came to dinner. They brought a cake. At first all the talk was about skating. There were many stories to tell. Azalea didn't say anything. She didn't have anything to say about skating. When they were having the cake, Glider mentioned dancing. Azalea said, "Dancing is the most wonderful thing in the world. I would rather dance than do anything else." Stari asked, "Who do you dance with?" Azalea said, "Before I met Glider, I danced only with very good dancers. I danced only with the best dancers. Now I dance with Glider." Stari asked, "Is he good enough?" Azalea said, "He is not the best dancer in the world. But I like to dance with him."

After Glider and Azalea left, Stari said, "Glider is much nicer than I thought. I like the way he talks about Flyer. He works very hard to teach Flyer. He believes that Flyer will be the best skater in the world someday. He may be right." Streamer asked, "And what about Azalea?" Stari said, "I didn't like her dress. She wears too much makeup. All she talks about is dancing. I bet she isn't going to be Glider's girlfriend very long. As soon as she meets a very good dancer, she will break up with Glider. She will go with the dancer." Streamer said, "This time, Stari, I'm not sure you are right."

One day, Glider was giving Flyer a skating lesson. He was teaching Flyer to jump. Flyer jumped. Glider could see that Flyer's body was turned the wrong way. Flyer was going to fall on his back. Glider didn't want Flyer to be hurt. He rushed up behind him, and caught him in the air. They both fell backward. Glider fell on the ice. Flyer fell on top of him. Flyer got up. Glider just lay on the ice. Flyer stretched out his arm to help Glider get up. Glider couldn't move. Glider was taken to the hospital.

At the hospital, Maya examined Glider. She also called other doctors to examine him. They took X-rays which show the inside of a person's body. They made many other tests. Glider had to stay in the hospital. The doctors and nurses said, "Go home, Azalea. Come back tomorrow." Azalea said, "No. I will not go home. I will not leave Glider alone. I will stay right here on a cot in his room. He will know that I am here if he needs anything."

Next day, Maya came to see Glider. Maya said, "I am very sorry, Glider. I have very bad news for you. You will never be able to use your legs again. You will have to use a wheelchair." Glider was very sad. He said, "I will never be able to walk again. I will never be able to dance again. I will never be able to skate again." And he cried.

Next morning, Maya came back to see him. She examined him. She listened to his heart. Then she said, "You came to see me once. I examined you. I thought you were sad. You had a one-five heartbeat. I have just examined you. I know you are sad. But you have a regular heartbeat. This is strange." Glider said, "No, Maya. I don't think it's strange. When I came to you, I was sad, but I didn't know I was sad, and I didn't want to admit I was sad. So I had a one-five heart beat. Now I'm sad. I know I'm sad, and I admit I'm sad. So I have a regular heartbeat. And there is another difference. When I came to you before, I was sad because I didn't want anything. So I didn't cry. Now I'm sad because I want many things that I'll never be able to have again. So I cry."

Maya said, "Let me give you some medicine. It will make you calm. And you won't have to cry." But Azalea said, "No, Maya. Glider doesn't need medicine to keep him from crying. Glider needs someone to cry with him." She put her head on his chest and hugged him. Maya said. "You are right, Azalea. I am only a doctor. There are times when doctors remember only what they learned in school. Right now, Azalea, you know more than I." She stroked Azalea's hair and left them alone.

Next day, Glider was brought home. He got a wheel chair. Many people came to visit him. He talked with them. He cried a lot. One day, Streamer and Stari came to visit. Azalea was happy to see them. Stari asked, "Do you ever go dancing, Azalea?" Azalea said, "Oh, no." Stari asked, "Don't you miss dancing?" Azalea said, "No. I don't miss it. Dancing was a wonderful part of my life. That is over now. If I cannot dance with Glider, I don't want to dance. I do other things." Stari asked, "What things?" Azalea said, "I go down to the river. There is a long path there. I run on that path. Each day I run a little further. Then I run back." Stari asked, "But why do you do this?" Azalea said, "When I run by the river, I'm all alone. There is nothing there. Only the river. Then I think. I think about how glad I am to be alive. I think about how glad I am that I'm Glider's girlfriend. Sometimes, I go to the hospital. There are sick children there. I take along books. I read to the children. Children like to have books read to them. That makes me happy."

Stari and Azalea became friends. They decided to make a party for Glider's birthday. They baked a birthday cake. They invited friends. Lark and Maya came. Mole came. Streamer and Stari came. Streamer's sister came. Stari's friend Lily came. Flyer came. Henna, Flyer's mother, came. Oaker and Ashly came. They all sat around the big table.

Lily asked Maya, "Is there any medicine that could make Glider better?" Maya said, "I don't know of any." Flyer's mother asked Maya, "Is there any operation that could make Glider better?" Maya said, "I don't know of any." Stari asked Ashly, "Is there any magic that could make Glider better?" Ashly said, "I don't know of any." Lark asked Oaker, "Is there any magic that could make Glider better?" Oaker said, "I don't know of any."

Then Mole said, "I have magic for Glider." Everyone was surprised. Mole never talked much. Streamer said to Mole, "I didn't know you believe in magic." Mole said, "This is difficult to explain. When I was small, I didn't believe in magic. Then one day, I thought I saw magic with my own eyes, so I changed my mind. Then I realized that I had been wrong, so I changed my mind again. Now I have changed my mind once more. I believe there are different kinds of magic. Some magic is high in the clouds. Some magic rests firmly on the ground. I am a shoemaker. I give Glider magic that rests firmly on the ground.

"Look at this coin. You might think it's an ordinary coin, but it isn't. When I started to make shoes, I wanted to make only shoes that fit perfectly. I could never do it. One day, I succeeded. The man who bought the shoes said, 'Yes. These shoes fit perfectly.' He paid me with this coin. Since then, all the shoes I have made have fit perfectly. From the moment I got this coin, I knew there was magic in it. I saved it for a day when I would need it. This day has come. This coin is my present to you.

"Now you must do exactly what I tell you. Two people must take you to the amusement park by the river." Both Oaker and Streamer immediately said, "I will go." Mole continued, "In the amusement park there is a roller coaster. You must use the magic coin to buy a ticket for a ride. Oaker and Streamer can help you get to the place where the tickets are sold. But you must buy the ticket yourself. They can lift you on one of the benches of the roller coaster. They cannot go along with you. They must choose a bench that is empty. No one can sit next to you. The bench in front of you must be empty. The bench behind you must be empty. It won't be hard to find such a bench. There aren't too many people in the amusement park at this hour. I know that Azalea and Stari have made a birthday cake for you. If Oaker and Streamer take you right now, we will wait here. We will have the birthday cake when you come back."

No one said anything. They didn't know what to say. Oaker and Streamer wheeled Glider out. The others remained where they were. They waited.

After an hour, Oaker and Streamer came back. Glider was still in the wheel chair. Stari asked, "What happened?" Streamer said, "We did exactly what Mole told us to do. Glider bought the ticket by himself. He used the magic coin to pay for it. He sat on a bench by himself. There was no one on the bench in front of him. There was no one on the bench behind him. He went on the ride by himself. When he came back, we told him to stand up. He tried to stand up. He couldn't. His legs didn't work. We lifted him into the wheel chair, and we came back. He didn't say a single word all the way back." Stari said, "I am sorry the magic didn't work." Maya said sadly, "I didn't believe the magic would work."

Then Glider said, "But it did work." Everyone was surprised. Glider said, "Thank you, Mole. You have given me a wonderful birthday present. Here is what happened. The roller coaster has three hills. The first one is small. The second one is bigger. The third one is gigantic. It's as big as a mountain. The car started to climb the first hill. I didn't pay much attention. I felt sorry for myself. Then we came to the top and started to fall. It was terrible. I was very frightened. I screamed and screamed until we came to the bottom. Then the car started to climb again.

"I realized that the second hill was much bigger than the first. I was frightened. I didn't want to be there. I cursed Mole. I cursed myself. I thought, why was I so stupid? Why did I agree to go? I screamed, 'I don't want to be here. Someone help me, please. Stop the roller coaster. I want to get off.' But no one was there. There was no one next to me. There was no one in front of me. There was no one behind me. I couldn't stop the roller coaster. I screamed all the way down the hill. Then the car started to climb again. This was the biggest hill of all. I realized that there was no way to get off. Then I said to myself, 'I will try to enjoy the ride.' It wasn't so bad. Actually it was fun.

"I didn't say anything to Oaker and Streamer. All the way back, I thought about my life. I am on a roller coaster now. There is no way to get off. But there are many things I can do. I can breathe fresh air. I can see the mountains. I can watch the sunrise. I can move around in my wheelchair. And I can be with Azalea, if she still wants me." Azalea said, "Of course, I want you." Glider said, "But I'm not a skater anymore." Azalea said, "Of course you are a skater. You will always be a skater. Flyer may grow up and become a bird flying across the ice. He may become the best skater in the world. I hope he will. But for me, you will always be the best skater that ever was." And Azalea hugged Glider.

Oaker said, "You're very lucky, Glider." Glider said, "I know. And I'm not the only one. Come here Flyer. You're lucky too. Until now, you've had only one teacher. From now on, you'll have two teachers. I have talked with Streamer. From now on, we'll both be your teachers." He hugged Flyer, and Flyer cried.

Then Glider continued. "I will learn to get around the skating rink on my wheelchair. There are many other things I can do. And then there is the most important thing I can do." He stopped. They all looked at him. No one said anything. Finally, Lark asked, "And what is that?" Glider said, "I can eat my birthday cake."

Azalea and Stari left the room. They came back with a big cake. It had many candles. The candles were burning brightly. They all sang "Happy Birthday." Then Glider blew out the candles. He blew them out with a single breath.

7. The Golden Handkerchief

Lark was a poet. He was married to Maya. She was a doctor. Their bedroom had a big window across an entire wall. There was a curtain in front of the window. During the day, when the curtain was open, they could see trees and meadows and big mountains in the distance. At night, when the curtain was closed, the room was dark, so Lark and Maya could sleep.

One night, Maya woke up. She felt Lark tossing on his side of the bed. She asked, "Are you awake, Lark?" Lark said, "Yes." Maya asked, "Why aren't you sleeping?" Lark said, "I couldn't sleep." Maya asked, "Is something the matter, Lark?" Lark said, "No." Maya asked, "Are you worried about something?" Lark said, "I'm not worried." Maya said, "I think you are worried about something. Please tell me what it is." Lark said, "No." Maya said, "You promised you would always tell me if you were worried about something." Lark said, "I'm ashamed to tell." Maya said, "You promised to tell even if you were ashamed." Lark said, "I remember." Maya said, "So, what is it?" Lark said, "I'm afraid."

Maya asked, "What are you afraid of?" Lark said, "I'm afraid of the dark." Maya asked, "How long have you been afraid of the dark?" Lark said, "I was afraid of the dark when I was small. I always slept with a light on in my room. When I grew up, I stopped being afraid. But since Glider's birthday party, I've been afraid again, just like when I was small." Maya said, "I wish you had told me sooner. Right now, we'll turn on the small light and keep it on. Will that help, Lark?" Lark said, "Oh, yes. That will help a lot. If the light is on, I won't be afraid." Maya said, "Good. That will take care of tonight. Tomorrow morning, I'll get medicine for you, so you won't have to be afraid anymore."

Lark said, "I know you're trying to help me, Maya. You're a doctor. You always want to give everyone medicine. But there are some things you can't fix with medicine. I'm a poet. I don't want to take medicine for the dark. It wouldn't be good for me. I will use another way." Maya said, "Please forgive me, Lark. I always make the same mistake."

Lark asked, "How about you, Maya? Were you ever afraid of the dark?" Maya said, "Yes. When I was a little girl, I was afraid of the dark. Then my mother gave me a big teddy bear. That's the one over there in the corner. I still keep it in our room. Since that time, I haven't been afraid of the dark." Lark said, "No one ever gave me a teddy bear. But I'm a poet. Tomorrow I will write a poem about being afraid. Perhaps this will help." Maya said, "I think this is a very good idea." They kept the little light on in the room.

Next morning, Maya went to work in the hospital. Lark didn't write the poem right away. He wanted to talk to other people first. He went to the skating rink. He asked Streamer, "Are you afraid of the dark?" Streamer said, "No." Lark asked, "Are you afraid of anything?" Streamer thought about it. Then he said, "No." Lark asked, "Nothing? Nothing at all?" Streamer said, "Well. Maybe. From the time Glider fell and hurt himself, maybe I've been afraid to jump."

Lark saw Flyer. Flyer was only 12 years old. Streamer and Glider were his skating teachers. Glider always said that Flyer would be the best skater in the world someday. Lark asked Flyer, "Are you afraid of the dark?" Flyer said, "No." Lark asked, "Are you afraid of anything?" Flyer said, "No." Lark said, "Glider was hurt when he jumped. Are you afraid you'll get hurt when you jump?" Flyer said, "No. I'm not afraid. If you're afraid, you can't jump." Lark asked, "Are you afraid of anything at all?" Flyer said, "Maybe one thing. I know how hard Glider works to teach me. Sometimes I wonder whether I'm as good as he says I am. Maybe I'm afraid of disappointing him."

Lark asked Stari, "Are you afraid of the dark?" Stari said, "No." Lark asked, "Are you afraid of anything?" Stari said, "No." Lark said, "You mean absolutely nothing at all?" Stari said, "Well, sometimes I am afraid Streamer will find another skating partner, Then he won't want to be married to me anymore."

Lark saw Glider in his wheelchair on the ice. Lark asked Glider, "Are you afraid of the dark?" Glider said, "No. But maybe I'm afraid of other things. There was a time when I said, I'm not afraid of anything. I didn't know I was afraid. And later when I knew I was afraid, I didn't want to admit it. I guess I'm afraid of being afraid."

Lark went to Mole's store. He asked Mole, "Are you afraid of the dark?" Mole said, "I don't think so." Lark asked, "Are you afraid of anything?" Mole said, "Yes. Both my parents died when I was small. No one ever took care of me. No one ever gave me a present. The bracelet you gave me was the first present I ever got. When I became a shoemaker, I wanted to make shoes that fit perfectly. I thought the people for whom I made the shoes would like me. But no one cared. Now I make shoes that fit perfectly because I want to make shoes that fit perfectly. I don't expect anymore that anyone will like me on account of the shoes. Yes, I am afraid. I'm afraid no one will ever like me. I'm afraid no one will ever want to marry me." Lark said, "I'm so sorry. Why didn't you ever tell me?" Mole said, "It never came up. Last night I dreamt of my own funeral. The coffin was there. But there were no people." Lark asked, "And what happened?" Mole said, "Nothing happened. That was the whole dream."

Lark said, "I've been thinking about visiting Oaker and Ashly. I want to ask them about being afraid. Why don't you come along." Mole said, "I would like to come along. I would like to hear what they say."

Lark went back home. He put paper on his desk. He put his pen on the paper. He sat down in the easy chair at the other end of the room. He thought about being afraid of the dark. Then he lifted his hand and pointed at the pen. The pen got up and wrote. When it was finished, Lark went over to the desk and read what the pen had written.

When Maya came home from the hospital, Lark said to her, "Today I wrote a poem about being afraid of the dark. Here it is." Maya read the poem. Then she said, "The poem is very good. But I'm surprised." Lark said, "I was surprised too." The poem was about an arrow and a target. The arrow was golden, and it was straight. It had a beginning. It had an end. The target was black, and it was round. It had no beginning. It had no end. The arrow hit the target and disappeared. The target was a black hole. It remained forever. Maya said, "It isn't a poem about being afraid of the dark. It's a poem about being afraid of dying."

On Saturday, Lark, Maya, and Mole climbed to the clearing where Oaker and Ashly's cabin was. Oaker and Ashly were happy to see them. They talked for a while. Then Lark said, "Ever since Glider's birthday party, I've been afraid of the dark. Maybe I'm not really afraid of the dark. Maybe I'm really afraid of dying. Is there any magic for being afraid?"

Ashly asked, "How about you, Maya? Are you afraid too?" Maya said, "I'm a doctor. I've seen many people die. Some have been afraid. Some have not been afraid. I've never understood why. I'm young and I don't think about it. But I can't be sure. Some people think they're not afraid, but when the time comes, they are. Other people think they're afraid, but when the time comes, they aren't."

Lark asked, "How about you Oaker? How about you Ashly? You are both much older than we are. Are you afraid of dying?" Oaker said, "Everyone is afraid of something. I am afraid. Ashly is afraid. But different people are afraid of different things. Ashly is younger than I. She is afraid that I will die. Then she won't have me anymore. I am afraid I may get sick and helpless. Then I won't be able to take care of myself anymore. These are the things we are afraid of. But we are not afraid of dying." Lark asked, "Were you ever afraid of dying?" Oaker said, "Yes, but the golden handkerchief changed that. From the time we got the golden handkerchief, neither Ashly nor I have ever been afraid of dying again." Maya asked, "What is the golden handkerchief?" Ashly said, "I will show it to you."

Ashly went into the other room and came back with a big handkerchief. Lark said, "But it isn't golden. It's black. I've never seen a handkerchief like this." Ashly spread the handkerchief out on the table and said, "It's not all black. The background is black. But look more closely, Lark." Lark took the handkerchief in his hand, and said, "Yes, there are fine golden threads woven into the black. There's a golden sun in the middle. And there are golden rays of light in all directions. I see why it's called the golden handkerchief." Mole asked, "What do you do with it?"

Oaker said, "Please pay careful attention." He told them that they had to go outside. He told them exactly what each of them had to do. Lark had to lie down. Maya had to cover his face with the golden handkerchief. Mole had to use a stopwatch. He had to say "start" and "stop" to make sure the golden handkerchief was on Lark's face exactly one minute, not more, not less. Except for Mole's saying "start" and "stop", no one was to say anything. They had to remain completely quiet the entire time, even after Maya had taken off the handkerchief from Lark's face. They had to wait, even if it took a long time. Oaker said, "Don't move after Maya has taken the handkerchief off Lark's face. Stay the way you are until Lark says something. I will explain later. Right now, just do exactly what I tell you to do."

Lark, Maya, and Mole had many questions. But they trusted Oaker. They didn't say anything. They went to the edge of the clearing. Lark lay down on the ground. Maya kneeled behind his head. She held the handkerchief at two corners. The handkerchief hung down. Its bottom edge just touched Lark's throat. Mole stood right behind her. He pushed the button on the watch, and said, "Start." Maya lowered her hands. The handkerchief fell over Lark's face. It covered his face completely. But she held on to the corners of the handkerchief. No one said anything.

The stopwatch was running. It ran for only one minute, but it seemed like a very long time to Maya. Then Mole said, "Stop." Maya pulled on the handkerchief so it no longer covered Lark's face. It hung down again, and touched Lark's throat again as it had when they started. For a long time, no one said anything. They were all waiting. Finally, Lark said, "Aren't you supposed to cover my face?" Maya said, "But we've already done that." Lark said, "I meant, didn't Oaker say you should start the watch, and that Maya should let the handkerchief fall right over my face?" Mole said, "Yes, but we've done that." Lark got up and said, "This is very strange. You are telling me things I know are not so. Perhaps it's magic. I don't understand it. Lets just go in and ask Oaker to explain."

They went inside, and Lark said to Oaker, " Maya and Mole tell me what they think happened, but I know what happened. If I didn't know better, I would think someone was trying to fool me. I don't understand it. Please explain it to me." Lark was surprised when Maya and Mole said, "Yes, Oaker. Please tell us what happened."

Oaker said, "No one tried to fool you, Lark. This wasn't a trick. Maya really put the golden handkerchief over your face, just like she said. You didn't know it, because when the golden handkerchief was put over your face, you died. For one whole minute, you were dead. You didn't know anything. You certainly didn't know that you were dead. You couldn't know. There was no one to know. Think about it, Lark. You'll never die. As long as there'll be a you, you'll be alive. You'll see other people die, but you won't die yourself. Perhaps you'll try to imagine being dead. But if you'll try, you'll do it all wrong, because one can only imagine something. One can't imagine nothing. Once you understand this, you'll never be afraid of dying again."

Lark, Maya and Mole thought and thought about this all the way back to town. Their heads were spinning. Sometimes, they thought they understood what Oaker had said. Then they didn't understand it again. But when Lark and Maya went to bed, Lark said, "Maya, please turn off the light. It's hard to sleep with the light on." She turned off the light, and a minute later Lark was fast asleep.

8. The Ruby Ring

One morning, Lark and Maya left their house together. Maya was a doctor. She was going to the hospital. Lark was a poet. He was going to the river. He wanted to walk by the river. He wanted to think about a new poem. When Maya had to turn off, they hugged and said goodbye. Lark went on alone. He was still far from the river, but he was already thinking about his poem. He just walked and thought. He didn't pay much attention to the street, or to the people on the street. He turned around a corner, and almost bumped into someone. He looked up. It was Featherman.

Featherman wore a dark blue shirt with many white stars on it, baggy purple pants, and a hat with a gigantic feather. Lark didn't know his name. He called him Featherman because of the feather. He was the man from the stall, where Lark had thrown three balls, and had won the count-down watch. Lark was surprised to see him suddenly right in front of him.

Featherman blocked Lark's way, and said, "Hello, hello, my friend. What's the matter with you? Don't you recognize me? Three balls for a dollar. Don't you remember?" Lark said, "Oh, yes, I remember. What happened to you?" Featherman said, "What do you mean, what happened to me?" Lark said, "I came back to look for you. You weren't there. The stall wasn't there. You disappeared."

Featherman said, "Don't be silly, my friend. A person can't just disappear. A stall can't just disappear. Who would believe a silly thing like this? You probably looked for me in the wrong place. I'm right here. I don't disappear. You can depend on it. But tell me, how is the count-down watch? I hope you are taking good care of it."

Lark didn't like the way the man talked to him, but the man was standing right in Lark's way. Lark couldn't go on. He said, "I lost it." Featherman cried out, "Oh no, you lost it. That's terrible. Didn't I tell you to take good care of it?" Lark said, "Well, I lost it. Now I must go. Goodbye." But he couldn't go. Featherman was blocking his way.

Featherman said, "What a shame. You lost your prize. Let me see. Let me see." He searched through his pockets, found something, and said, "Here. Take this instead. You won a prize. You must have a prize. This is a very good prize. It is a ruby ring." He pushed the ring into Lark's hand. It was a gold ring with a small red stone. Featherman said, "This is a very special ring, and you are very lucky to get this prize." Lark said, "But I didn't do anything to get a prize." Featherman said, "Yes, you did. You hit three cans. You lost your first prize. So you get a second prize. Most people don't get even one prize. You get two. Now you have a ruby ring. I bet you don't know what a ruby ring is. I bet you don't know what a ruby ring can do."

Now Lark was curious. He asked, "What can it do?" Featherman stepped closer, and whispered, "If you touch someone with the ruby ring, they like you." Lark said, "Is that all? People like me. I don't need a ruby ring." The man shook his head and said, "No, no, no. Not just like you. If you wear the ruby ring, and touch someone with it, they like you very much. Much, much, much. You see? Much, much, much. Just think. You see a pretty lady. You touch her with the ruby. You see?"

Lark said, "I have a wife." Featherman said, "Yes. Everybody has a wife. But this has nothing to do with it." Lark said, "I don't want your ring. Here, take it back." Featherman put both his hands behind his back, and said, "No. The ring is yours. Now you must give me a dollar." Lark said, "Why?" Featherman said, "That's how it is. Remember? Three balls for a dollar. You pay a dollar. You get a prize. Now you must give me a second dollar for the second prize." Lark said, "But I don't want the prize." Featherman said, "Let's not argue about it. Give me a dollar, so I can go. I'm very busy."

Lark wanted to get away from the man. He gave him a dollar. The man took the dollar and said, "Very good. And just one more thing. You must always wear the ring." Lark cried out, "What do you mean, always?" Featherman said, "If you touch someone with the ring, they will like you very much. Much, much, much. Right? Right. But if you take off the ring, it's over. They won't like you much, much, much anymore."

Lark asked, "Will they like me less than before?" Featherman said, "No. If you take off the ring, they will like you the same as before. Not less. Not more. Only the same. That's not much. So, don't take off the ring. You see. That's how it is. But I can't stand here, talking with you all day. I have to go. I have a lot to do. Good luck with the ring. Goodbye." And Featherman hurried away.

Lark put the ring in his pocket. He wondered whether the ring really worked. Then he began to think about the poem he wanted to write, and he forgot about the ring. The poem was about a mountain and a river. The mountain always stayed the same. The river always changed. Together, they filled up the whole world.

When Lark came home, he sat down in his easy chair, and pointed at his pen. The pen wrote the poem. When it was finished, Lark read the poem. He liked the poem. Then he remembered the ring. He put the ring on his finger and waited for Maya. When Maya came home, he said to her, "Maya, I have written a new poem. Please read it." He gave her the poem. At the same time, he touched her with the ring.

Maya read the poem. She said, "It is a good poem." Lark asked, "Do you like me, Maya? I mean, do you like me very much?" Maya laughed and said, "Don't be silly, Lark. You know that you are my everything." Then Maya noticed the ring, and asked, "Oh, where did you get this ring?"

Lark never lied to Maya. He thought it was very bad to lie to one's wife. But he didn't want to tell her everything about the ring. So he said, "I bought the ring from a man on the street." This was true. It was not perhaps the whole truth, but it was certainly not a lie.

Lark took the ring off his finger, and put it into his pocket. He gave Maya a big hug, and asked, "Tell me, Maya. Did you like me better before?" Maya asked, "Before when?" Lark said, "Before. When you read my poem." Maya said, "You're being very silly today, Lark. I liked your poem. I'm glad you can write good poems. But I didn't like you more when you gave me your poem. And if you wrote a bad poem, which is of course impossible, I wouldn't like you less. I always like you the same. Because you are my everything."

That evening, Lark went to the Parlor to read his new poem. The Parlor is a place with round tables and chairs, where people sit, eat, drink, and talk with their friends. There is also a little platform. Whenever Lark wrote a new poem, he stood on the platform. When people saw him, they stopped talking. When it was all quiet in the room, Lark read his poem.

This evening, four young people sat at a table not far from the platform. One young woman was doing all the talking. Her friends listened. Then they laughed. Perhaps she was telling jokes. Right away, Lark didn't like her. He didn't like her face. He didn't like the expression on her face. He didn't like the way her hair was fixed. Mostly, he didn't like that she was talking very loudly. He didn't know her name, but in his mind he called her Loudmouth.

Lark went up the steps, and stood on the platform. Soon most people in the room stopped talking. They were waiting for Lark to begin. Loudmouth kept on talking. The people at her table kept on laughing. Lark waited. Lark was very particular about reading his poems. He thought his poems were very important. He wanted the room to be completely quiet before he started to read. He didn't want anyone to do anything while he read. He wanted everyone to pay attention. Loudmouth wouldn't stop. Now she was whispering. The people at her table had to lean forward to hear her. But it was still not completely quiet.

Finally, Lark couldn't wait any longer. He began to read. Loudmouth didn't pay attention. She giggled. She made her friends giggle. Lark thought she was making jokes about his poem. When Lark finished reading, the people in the room clapped a lot. They liked Lark's poem. Loudmouth didn't clap. Her friends clapped only a little. Lark was very angry.

When he stepped down from the platform, Lark remembered that he still had the ruby ring in his pocket. He put it on his finger, and walked back to his own table. When he passed behind Loudmouth, he touched her back with the ruby for a moment. Loudmouth turned around and looked up at him. Lark said, "Excuse me," and he went on to his table.

Next morning, there was a knock on the door of Lark's house. Loudmouth was there. Her hair was combed. She wore a nice dress and gold ear rings. Lark could smell perfume. She said, "I'm so sorry to disturb you. My name is Lila. May I come in?" Lark said, "Come in." Lila said, "I'm a reporter for the newspaper. I was at the Parlor yesterday, and I heard you read your poem. It was wonderful." Lark said, "Really? You liked it?" Lila said, "I didn't just like it. I want to write a story about it for the newspaper." Lark said, "I thought maybe you didn't hear all of it. I saw you whispering with your friends." Lila said, "Oh yes. I was whispering. Your lines were so good, I wanted to make sure my friends understood them."

Lark asked, "Which lines did you like?" Lila said, "The way you described the mountain. From now on, I will think of the mountain in a new way." Lark said, "Please don't just stand. Please sit down. Yes, I think I described the mountain very well. I'm glad you liked it." Lila said, "And of course it wasn't just the mountain. There was the river. The way you put the river together with the mountain was wonderful."

Lark asked, "You really think so?" Lila said, "Of course, I think so. I wouldn't say it if I didn't. I always tell the truth, even when people don't want to hear it. That's best. Don't you think?" Lark looked at Lila. She was much prettier than he remembered from last night. He said, "Yes. The truth is best. That's what a poem tries to do. It tries to help us remember things we know, but don't know we know." Lila said, "This is very good. I'll use it when I write my story about you. I'll have to hear more. I'll have to come back. Maybe not just one time. Maybe two times. Maybe three times. Is there any poem I could hear right now?" Lark said, "I wrote a poem about dying." Lila asked, "Did you read it at the Parlor?" Lark said, "I didn't. I thought maybe people wouldn't like to hear a poem about dying." Lila said, "I would like to hear a poem about dying. Why don't you read it to me right now." Lark said, "I'll get it. Please wait right here."

Lark went into the other room. The poem about dying was in the drawer of the table. As he picked it up, he saw the glasses Oaker and Ashly had given him and Maya as a wedding present. Through these glasses, one could see the strands of light between his heart and Maya's heart. For a moment, Lark wanted to pick up the glasses and take a quick look. But he didn't pick up the glasses. He was afraid to look. Instead, he took off the ruby ring, and put it into his pocket. He picked up the poem about dying and went into the other room.

Lila was standing. She said, "I'm sorry. I forgot. I have an appointment. I must leave." Lark asked, "Don't you want to hear my poem about dying?" Lila said, "Not now. You'll probably read it at the Parlor sometime. I'll hear it then." Lark asked, "And how about the story for your newspaper?" Lila said, "I'm only a reporter. The editor decides what stories are put into the newspaper. I'll tell him about you. Now I must go. Goodbye."

After Lila left, Lark thought, the ruby ring is real, just like the count-down watch. Oaker said the count-down watch could be a good thing or a bad thing. It depends on who has it, and on what the person does with it. It's probably the same with the ruby ring. It could be a good thing or a bad thing. It depends on who has it, and on what the person does with it. I don't need the ruby ring. I may not use it wisely. I could throw it away, like Maya threw away the count-down watch. But Mole might be able to use it. Mole is afraid no one likes him. He's afraid no one will ever want to marry him. Perhaps the ruby ring will help him. I'll give it to Mole.

Lark went to visit Mole. They talked for a while. Then Lark said, "This is a ruby ring. It's a real ruby ring. I know it works. When you wear this ring, and touch someone with it, that person will like you. That person will not just like you a little. That person will like you a lot. There's only one thing. You can't take off the ring." Mole asked, "What do you mean, I can't take off the ring? " Lark said, "Of course, you can take off the ring. But if you take it off, anyone you touched with it, will like you no more than they did when you first touched them."

Mole said, "I don't know whether I want anyone to like me just because I touch them with a ring." Lark said, "I know Mole. It's magic. But magic can be good. Keep the ring. You don't have to use it. Keep it, just in case." Mole took the ring and put it into the drawer where he kept his tools.

A few days later, a young woman came into Mole's store. She wore torn shoes, no makeup, no necklace, no earrings. She said, "My name is Henna. I think I need new shoes." Mole said, "I think you do. How long is it since you got new shoes?" Henna said, "It is many years. I haven't had any money. Do you think I could pay for the shoes just a little each week?" Mole said, "That's all right. You probably need other things too."

Henna told Mole her story. She was married to a man named Wolf. He killed animals in the forest. Henna didn't like it when Wolf killed animals. They had a child, a little boy. Wolf didn't want to stay with Henna and help her take care of the little boy. Wolf went away to another town. Henna went to a judge. The judge asked Wolf to come back. Wolf didn't come. The judge said that Henna and Wolf were divorced. The judge said that Wolf should send money for the little boy. But Wolf didn't send any money, and Henna had very little money.

Mole said, "I'll make you shoes that fit perfectly. And you can pay me whatever you can each week. But why did you marry Wolf?" Henna said, "It was a mistake. I was very young. My mother wanted me to marry Wolf. I didn't know how mean he was. And then I stayed with him because of my little boy. I have very little money now. But I'm very glad I'm not married to Wolf anymore."

Mole liked everything about Henna. She looked plain, but Mole thought she was beautiful. He wanted her to like him too. He didn't think anyone would ever like him. Then he remembered the ruby ring. He said, "Stand on this cardboard. I will measure your feet, so I can make you shoes that fit perfectly." He opened the drawer. He took out his tools. He also took out the ruby ring and put it on his finger. He drew the outline of Henna's feet on the cardboard. He touched Henna with the ruby. Then he said, "Your shoes will be ready next week."

Henna said, "Would it be all right if I came back before next week?" Mole said, "But your shoes won't be ready yet." Henna said, "Yes, I know. But I often walk by the river. I thought that, if you like the river too, maybe we could walk there together." Mole said, "I would very much like to walk by the river with you."

After that, Henna and Mole went walking by the river every day. At first, Henna walked in her old, torn shoes. But after a week, she picked up her new shoes. They fit perfectly. She always came to Mole's store. At first, she came late in the afternoon, so Mole had time to work all day. Then she came earlier. Each day she came a little earlier. She said, "Please, Mole, don't stop. Please go on working. I just like to sit here and watch. I like to see you making shoes." Then Mole went on working while Henna watched. Henna was happy and Mole was happy.

Mole told Lark about Henna. He told him that he liked her very much. He told him that he had touched her with the ruby ring. Lark said, "I'm glad you are happy, Mole. But please listen to me. Whatever you do, don't take off the ruby ring." Mole asked Lark, "Is it fair that I used magic on Henna?" And Lark said, "Yes, it is fair, Mole. I am your friend. Trust me. I am very sure it's all right. Magic must be judged by its results. No one is being hurt. Henna is happy. You are happy. This magic has had only good results. Don't take off the ring."

One day, when they were walking by the river, Mole said to Henna, "I think you know I like you very much" Henna said, "I'm happy you say this, Mole, because I like you very much too. I like you as much as the mountain is high." Then Mole said, "I want you to come and live with me in my house. And, if you want, we could get married." Henna said, "There's nothing in the world I would like better, Mole. But I have a son." Mole said, "I know that. I want you both to come. My house is big enough." And Henna said, "It would be wonderful if we could all live together. I'll talk with my boy tonight." Mole gave Henna a very big hug.

They went on walking together along the river. They held hands. They felt close. They didn't talk. Henna had her thoughts. Mole had his thoughts. Mole thought about the ruby ring. He thought: Henna is wonderful. I am ordinary. She was married to Wolf. When she found out who he really was, she didn't like him. He wasn't what he seemed. It was all a mistake. Maybe I am like Wolf. I am not what I seem. I made her like me with magic. When she finds out who I really am, maybe she will not like me anymore. Maybe she will think that this too was a mistake.

When he had this thought, Mole took off the ring. With all his strength, he threw the ring into the river. Henna asked, "What was that?" Mole said, "Nothing, Henna. I just threw away something I didn't want anymore."

Then Mole stopped and stood right in front of Henna. He looked into her eyes, and said, "Look at me Henna. Please look at me. Tell me, do you still like me?" Henna said, "I can't understand why you ask such a foolish question, Mole. Of course I like you. I like you very much. I like you as much as the mountain is high." Mole asked, "Did you like me this much right away? I mean, when you first saw me, the day you came into my store, when I measured your feet?" And Henna said, "But this is not when I first saw you. Didn't you recognize me, Mole? Don't you know who I am? Don't you remember?"

Mole was surprised. He asked, "What do you mean?" Henna said, "The first time I saw you was at Glider's birthday party. I thought you remembered. I am Flyer's mother. Flyer is my boy. Glider was very sad. He needed magic. You gave him the magic coin. You told us that there are two kinds of magic, magic that is high in the clouds, and magic that rests firmly on the ground. When I heard this, I knew that, after all these years, I had found a good man, an honest man, a wise man, a handsome man. From that moment on, I liked you as much as the mountain is high." Mole asked, "So you liked me already when you came to my store?" And Henna said, "Of course. That's why I came. I wore torn shoes for a long time. I could have worn them longer. I didn't come for the shoes. I wanted to see you again. That's why I came." Mole gave Henna another big hug, and said, "I am happier than I have ever been in my whole life."

The next time Lark saw Mole, he saw that Mole wasn't wearing the ruby ring. He was worried, and asked, "Did you use the ruby ring?" Mole said, "Yes, I did." Lark asked, "Did the magic work?" Mole said, "Yes, it did." Lark asked, "What happened to the ring?" Mole said, "I threw it into the river." Lark asked, "When you threw the ring into the river, did the magic stop?" Mole answered, "No. That's when the magic started." And he smiled.

9. The Glitter Plate

One day Lila came to Lark's house. Lila was a reporter for the newspaper. First, she said she wanted to write a story about Lark and his poems. Then she said only the editor could put a story into the newspaper.

After Lila left, Lark began to think about a story in the newspaper. He imagined the story. Perhaps the newspaper would print one of his poems. Perhaps it would print a picture of him. Lark had always liked people to pay attention to him. He thought if there was a picture of him in the newspaper, people would pay a lot of attention to him. Everybody would recognize him. People would say, "This is Lark, the poet they wrote about in the newspaper." The more he thought about the idea, the better he liked it.

Lila had said she would tell the editor about Lark. At first, Lark was going to wait until the editor came to him. But the editor didn't come. After a few days, Lark became impatient. He didn't want to wait any longer. He wanted to see his picture in the newspaper. He wanted to see it soon. He said to himself, "Why should I wait for the editor to come. Perhaps he's doing other things. If I wait too long, he may forget me. I won't wait for him to come to me. I'll go to him."

Next day, Lark went to the newspaper building. It was a big building. People were rushing around. There were reporters, and proofreaders, and typesetters, and big machines on which the newspaper was printed. The editor was the big boss of the newspaper. His name was Haggler. Haggler was very busy. Lark had to wait a long time to see him. Finally, a secretary took Lark into Haggler's office. It was a big office. Haggler sat behind a big desk.

Lark said, "You have a reporter by the name of Lila." Haggler said, "Yes." Lark asked, "Has Lila spoken to you about me? My name is Lark. I'm a poet." Haggler said, "No. She hasn't said anything." Lark said, "Lila told me maybe you would put a story about me into the newspaper." Haggler looked surprised, and said, "But I've never heard of you." Lark said, "I usually read my poems in the Parlor." Haggler said, "Are you the fellow who stands on the platform and waits until everyone is quiet?" Lark said, "That's right. That's me."

Haggler said, "I never go to the Parlor, but I was there once. Someone read a poem. It was about a roller coaster. I don't remember the poem. But I remember thinking it was a very good poem. I sat way in back of the room. I couldn't see much. Was that you?"

Lark said, "Yes, that was me. I'm happy you liked my poem. So will you put a story about me in your newspaper?" Haggler exclaimed, "A story about you? That's impossible." Lark said, "I thought since you liked my poem, you would want to put a story into your newspaper." Haggler said, "I liked your poem. But this has nothing to do with it. Don't you know that we only put stories in the newspaper about people who are famous. And you're not famous." Lark said, "How do you know I'm not famous?" Haggler smiled, and said, "It's obvious you don't know much about the newspaper business. Maybe you don't know much about anything else either. Perhaps this is all right, because you are a poet. A poet doesn't have to know much. All a poet has to do is put words together. But I liked your poem, so I will help you."

Haggler got up. He walked over to a closet and opened the door. The closet was full of white things, stacked high. Lark couldn't tell what they were. Haggler took one of the white things from the top. He closed the door of the closet, and came back. He sat down behind his desk. He put the white thing on his desk, and said, "Look at this, and tell me what you think it is."

Lark looked at the white thing. It was a plate, a saucer for a teacup. On the top side, there was a circle with a rim around it where one could put the teacup. And there was a round base on the underside. Lark turned it over twice. He looked at it from all sides. He said, "It looks like a plate to me. I think it's a saucer for a teacup. It looks like an ordinary plate to me." Haggler started to laugh. Then he said, "Whatever it is, it's certainly not an ordinary plate." He lowered his voice, and said, "It's a glitter plate."

Lark asked, "What's a glitter plate?" Haggler took the plate and turned it face down. He took a crayon, and wrote "Lark" on the underside of the plate. He said, "I'm writing with a glitter crayon. When you use a glitter crayon to write a name on a glitter plate, that name can never be erased. It remains there as long as the plate remains. Now you have a glitter plate of your own. Turn it over, and see for yourself."

Lark turned over the plate. He was surprised. Inside the circle where the cup would go, there was a number that hadn't been there before. The number was 128. It was very bright blue." Lark asked, "How did this number get here?" Haggler laughed again, and said, "Aha. Now we don't think that this is such an ordinary plate anymore, do we? Just go over there, away from the window and look at it more closely."

Lark stepped away from the window and looked. He said, "The number glows." Haggler laughed again, and said, "Yes. Now we see that it glows. It isn't so ordinary anymore, is it?" Lark said, "That's right." Haggler said, "Now you see why I can't put a story about you in the newspaper." Lark said, "I don't see anything." Haggler said, "I don't know about that. But you certainly don't see much. 128 is your glitter count. At least it was your glitter count when you first looked at your glitter plate. Look again now."

Lark looked at the plate. The glowing number had changed. Lark said, "It was 128 before. It's 127 now. But what does this mean? And who cares?" Once again, Haggler laughed, and said, "Who cares? I'll tell you who cares. You care. That's who cares. Your glitter count is the number of people who thought about you during the past week, during the past seven days, exactly seven days, down to the minute, down to this very moment, as we speak." Lark said, "127 people? That's a lot of people, isn't it?" Haggler shook his head sadly, and said, "127 people is very few people. Your glitter count isn't worth anything until it's 1000."

Lark exclaimed, "1000? Isn't that a very big number?" Haggler said, "For ordinary people, this may be a big number. But for us at the newspaper, even 1000 is a small number. If your glitter count is less than 1000, it means you're not famous. If you're not famous, there can't be a story about you in the newspaper. Understand? If you want a story in the newspaper, you must first have a glitter count of 1000 or more."

Lark cried out, "But how? I don't see how this can be done." Haggler said, "Don't get so excited. Has anyone ever told you that you're very impulsive? Take it easy. I said I'll help you, and I will. But let me ask you a few questions first.

How often do you read a poem at the Parlor?" Lark thought about it for a moment. Then he said, "It could be once a week, sometimes twice a week. It depends." Haggler said, "It depends? That's not the right answer. What does it depend on?" Lark said, "It depends on whether I have a new poem." Haggler said, "There's no such thing as it depends. You must read a new poem every day." Lark cried out, "Every day? I may not have a new poem every day." Haggler said, "It doesn't matter whether you have a new poem. If you don't have one, make one." Lark said, "The poem may not be good." Haggler said, "It doesn't matter whether the poem is good. You want people to think of you, don't you? You want to be famous, don't you?" Lark said, "People may think badly of me." Haggler said, "It doesn't matter how they think of you, as long as they think of you. And another thing. Do your poems rhyme?" Lark said, "Sometimes they do. Sometimes they don't."

Haggler said, "From now on, make your poems rhyme all the time." Lark cried out, "Why?" Haggler said, "Because you want to be famous. That's why. And another thing. Are your poems funny?" Lark said, "No. Why should they be funny?" Haggler said, "Why, why, why, that's all you ask, just like a little child. I'm trying to help you, and you keep on asking why. Your poems should rhyme, because people like poems that rhyme. Your poems should be funny, because people like poems that are funny. That's why."

When Lark thought of a new poem, he usually let his pen write down the poem by itself. He wasn't sure his pen would write down every single day funny poems that rhyme. He didn't think writing such poems would be much fun. He wasn't sure he wanted to do this.

Suddenly, Lark was very sad. He said, "When I read my poems in the Parlor, the people always clap." Haggler shook his head, and said, "I'm afraid you still don't get it. They clap? What has that gotten you? 127. That's what it's gotten you. I'm trying to help you, and all you do is argue with me. Here, take along your glitter plate, and think about it. If you don't care whether you're famous, I don't care either. But if you want to be in the newspaper, maybe with a picture, you'll have to learn a thing or two. The only reason I'm spending so much time with you is because I liked your poem about the roller coaster. Now I've done all I can to help you. I've told you what I think. The rest is up to you. Good luck."

When he left Haggler's office, Lark was unhappy and confused. For a while he thought that maybe he shouldn't try to be famous. But he kept on thinking about the story in the newspaper. He imagined that the story would have a big picture of him. Then he thought, "Haggler is the editor of a big newspaper. He knows more about these things than I."

Next day, Lark went for a walk by the river. He wanted to think about a new poem. But all he could think about was how his picture would look in the newspaper. First, he thought the picture should be on top of the page. Then he thought the picture should be on the bottom of the page. Then he thought the picture should be right in the middle of the page. And the story should be all around the picture.

When he came home, he sat down in his easy chair, as he always did. After a while, he pointed at the pen, as he always did. Usually, the pen got up and started to write all by itself. Now, nothing happened. The pen just lay on the paper. Lark pointed a second time. The pen didn't move. Finally, Lark went to his desk. He picked up the pen and started to write with it himself. He wrote for a while. Then he crossed out what he had written. He wrote some more. Again he crossed out what he had written. Finally, he finished the poem.

When Maya came home from the hospital, Lark asked her to read his new poem. Maya read it, but didn't say anything. Lark asked, "What do you think?" Maya said, "It's different from the other poems you've written." Lark asked, "Yes. But what do you think of it?" Maya said, "Maybe you need to work on this poem some more." Lark said, "I don't have time to work on this poem. I have to read it at the Parlor tonight." Maya asked, "Why?" Lark said, "Because Haggler, the editor of the newspaper, says he'll put a story about me in the newspaper if I read a poem every day." Maya asked, "Why is it so important to have a story in the newspaper?" Lark said, "The story will have a picture of me." Maya said, "Maybe it doesn't matter whether there's a picture of you in the newspaper." But Lark just shook his head. He couldn't stop thinking about the picture.

After that, Lark did not sit in his easy chair and point at the pen anymore. The pen did not write by itself anymore. Lark sat at his desk. He held the pen, and he wrote everything himself. He wrote only poems with rhymes. He tried to write poems that were funny. People didn't always think the poems were funny. He wrote a new poem every day. He read it at the Parlor every evening. People didn't clap as much. But he looked at the glitter plate, and saw that Haggler had been right. Every day, the number on the glitter plate was a little higher. It got to be as high as 214, but Lark was sad.

At first, Lark was just a little sad. Then he became more sad. Maya asked, "What's the matter, Lark?" Lark said, "I'm sad. I'm very sad." Maya asked, "Why are you sad?" Lark said, "I don't know. I'm getting sadder and sadder all the time." Lark stopped walking to the river. He stopped going out of the house. He stopped going to the Parlor. The number on his glitter plate was lower again. He didn't care. Maya asked, "Are you afraid of something?" Lark said, "No." Maya asked, "Do you want to visit Mole and talk with him?" Lark said, "No." Maya asked, "Would you like me to bake you a chocolate cake?" Lark said, "I don't care. I don't want anything. I don't want to do anything. I don't want to go anywhere." And Lark began to cry.

Maya said, "Lark, dear Lark, I'm worried about you. I think maybe you are sick. I want you to come to the hospital." Lark said, "I'm not going to the hospital." Maya said, "Look at me, Lark. Dear, dear Lark, please do this for me. You don't have to stay in the hospital long. Just two hours maybe. I want to examine you. I want to do some tests. I want to make sure you're not sick." Lark said, "No medicine." Maya said, "I promise. No medicine. Only tests." Lark said, "All right."

Lark went to the hospital with Maya. A nurse brought Lark to a small room. There was a table with a sheet on it. The table could be raised or lowered. The nurse said, "First, take out everything you have in your pockets, so nothing will be lost. Put all your things on this shelf. Then take off your clothes. You can keep on your underwear. But take off everything else. Then lie down on this table, and wait. I'll be back." She left the room and closed the door.

Lark started to take out everything from his pockets. He didn't have much. There was a comb. There were his keys. And there was the glitter plate. He always carried it with him. When he took out the glitter plate, he looked at the number. It was 96. Lark turned the plate around. The number was still 96. Right side up or upside down, 96 was always the same. He turned the plate a few times. When he did this, he remembered a trick he could do when he was a little boy.

Children know things that grown ups don't. That's because grownups often forget things they knew when they were children. Poets are different. Even when they are grown up, they remember things they knew when they were children. Now Lark remembered that, when he was small, he could make a plate spin. He could throw it up in the air, and he could catch it on one finger, while it kept on spinning. It didn't work all the time, of course, but it was exciting when it did.

Now he wanted to see whether he could still do it. He spun the plate very hard. He threw it into the air, and caught it on his finger. He threw it higher, and caught it again. He was happy that he could still do the trick. He threw the plate higher. He didn't worry about the plate. He threw the plate even higher. He wondered how high he could throw it. Just then, the plate slipped. It fell to the floor and broke. Lark thought it would break into two or three pieces, but it broke into many fine pieces, as fine as dust. The dust just flew away. There was nothing left to pick up.

The moment the plate hit the floor, Lark was happy. He no longer cared whether he was famous. He no longer cared whether his picture was in the paper. He no longer wanted the magic of the glitter plate. He was sure he knew what he really wanted. He just wanted to let his pen write whatever it wrote.

Lark thought to himself, Oaker is very wise. Oaker said magic could be a good thing or a bad thing. It depends on who uses it and for what. Someday, Lark hoped, he would be wise enough to use magic the right way. He knew he wasn't wise enough yet. But he was happy now. He thought he was wise enough to know that he wasn't wise enough.

Lark started to get dressed. The nurse came in and said, "Why are you putting on your clothes? I'm ready to do the tests." Lark said, "I don't need the tests." The nurse said, "You can't leave. Wait here. I will call the doctor."

Maya came in. Lark said to her, "Look at me, Maya. I'm not sad anymore. I'm happy now. You can tell. I don't need any medicine, and I don't need any tests." Maya looked at him and said, "Yes, Lark. I can tell. But how did you get better?" Lark smiled and said, "This is a hospital, isn't it? People come here to get better, don't they? Well, I came here, and got better. So why are you surprised?"

Lark left the hospital. He went for a walk by the river. He thought of a poem. When he came back home, he sat down in his easy chair. He pointed at the pen. The pen got up and wrote all by itself. When the pen had finished, Lark read what the pen had written, and nodded. It was a poem about a bird and a meadow. The bird flew high over the meadow. The meadow was black. The bird flew lower. It saw a small golden sun in the middle of the meadow. There were golden rays going out in all directions. The bird flew lower. The sun was bigger. The bird flew lower still. The sun filled the whole world.

That evening, Lark read his poem to the people in the Parlor. The people liked Lark's poem. They clapped a long time. When Lark stepped down from the platform, a man came up to him. It was Haggler. He said, "I see you're ignoring my advice. I guess you don't want to have your picture in the newspaper. But I have to say one thing. That was a very good poem. Yessir, that was a very, very good poem." Lark said, "I'm glad you liked it."

10. The Pass-Along Anniversary

One Saturday, there was a knock on the door of Lark and Maya's house. Lark opened the door. He was surprised to see Oaker and Ashly. They lived in a cabin half way up the mountain. They did not come to town very often. Lark was happy to see them. He asked them to come in.

Oaker said, "We have come to invite you to a party in our cabin next week." Lark asked, "Is it a birthday party?" Oaker said, "No. It's an anniversary party." Maya asked, "How long have you been married?" Ashly said, "It isn't that kind of anniversary. It's Oaker's twenty-fifth pass-along anniversary." Lark asked, "What's a pass-along anniversary?" Oaker smiled, and said, "Come to my party and find out." Maya said, "Of course, we'll come."

Oaker said, "Now we'll go to invite Mole and Henna." Lark and Maya said they wanted to come along. The four of them went to Mole and Henna's house. Mole was happy to see them. Oaker invited Mole and Henna to come to his party. Henna asked, "Can Flyer come too?" Ashly said, "Of course."

Oaker said, "Now we'll go to invite Streamer and Stari." Mole and Henna wanted to come along. They all went to Streamer and Stari's house. Streamer and Stari were happy to see them. Oaker invited them to come to his party. Stari said, "We'll certainly come. But what is a pass-along anniversary?" Ashly said, "Come to the party and find out."

Oaker said, "Now we'll go to invite Glider and Azalea." Streamer said, "Glider is in a wheelchair. How will he get to the party?" Stari said, "We'll figure out a way. I'm sure we can do it." All of them went to Glider and Azalea's house. Oaker said, "We have come to invite you to a pass-along anniversary party. Will you come?" Azalea asked, "Where is the party?" Oaker said, "At our cabin." Glider said, "I would like to come. But I won't be able to get up to your cabin in my wheelchair." Stari said, "Don't worry about it, Glider. We'll get you up there. Just leave it to me." Azalea gave Stari a big hug, and said, "Thank you, Stari. You are a good friend. Most people would have said it can't be done." Stari said, "There are many things people say can't be done. But if you want to do them, they can be done." Stari wasn't wearing the forgetting chain anymore. But she still forgot that things can't be done.

Next Saturday, they all came to Glider and Azalea's house. Stari took charge. She told Glider to start out in his wheelchair. The others walked in front and behind the wheelchair until they came to the end of the meadow where the wild flowers are. There, the road became too rough for the wheelchair. Stari said, "We'll make two teams. Lark, Maya, Streamer and I will start." They had brought along two broomsticks. They passed the broomsticks under the seat of the wheelchair from front to back. Lark held the two broomsticks in front. Streamer held them in back. Maya held the left arm of the wheelchair. Stari held the right arm. Glider held on to the broomsticks to keep from sliding back and forth. They went up for a while. Then Mole, Henna, Flyer and Azalea took over. The two teams took turns. They stopped to rest often. It took longer than usual, but they got to the clearing. From there, they could see the town far below. They could look across to the mountains in the distance.

Oaker and Ashly were outside waiting for them. Oaker held a short stick in his hand. After they had rested for a while, Oaker said, "Come closer, all of you, and look. This stick is not an ordinary stick. It's a wishing rod." He raised the wishing rod, and said, "Honorable wishing-helper, please come." They were all surprised to see a man step out from behind a tree. They couldn't understand why they hadn't seen him before. The man wore dark blue pants and a dark blue shirt with gold buttons. He walked over to Oaker. He stood directly in front of him, and said, "Dear friend, what is your wish?" Oaker said, "I wish to have lunch for my friends." The wishing-helper said, "Your wish is granted, dear friend."

The wishing-helper went behind the cabin. He came back with a woman, two boys, and two girls. The woman was dressed the same way as the man. The boys and girls were also dressed the same way. But instead of long pants, they wore shorts. They carried a big table. They put down the table in the shade, at the edge of the clearing. They brought chairs. They brought dishes, spoons, forks, knives. They brought platters with food. There was a large bowl of salad. There was a plate with different cheeses. There was a plate with different kinds of fish, white fish, smoked salmon, herring, shrimp, anchovies. There was a plate with tomatoes, onions, and many kinds of olives. There were baskets with breads, white bread with a crunchy crust, rolls, bagels, whole wheat bread, dark bread. There were bowls of fruit, with apples, pears, peaches, nectarines, grapes, pineapples, strawberries, raspberries, blueberries. And there were things to drink, mineral water, sodas, orange juice, grapefruit juice, apple juice, red wine and white wine.

Azalea asked, "Are the boys and girls wishing-helpers too?" Ashly answered, "The woman is a wishing-helper, just like the man. The boys and the girls are assistants. They will be wishing-helpers when they grow up. Maya asked, "Where do the wishing-helpers come from? Where do they live?" Oaker answered, "I don't know. All I know is that when I call them with the wishing rod, they always come." Mole asked, "How long have you had the wishing rod?" Oaker said, "Exactly twenty-five years today. But let's have our lunch first. We'll talk later."

Everyone liked the food. After they finished eating, they remained sitting at the table. The sun was shining brightly, but the table was in the shade of the trees, and a cool breeze was blowing. They felt very good.

Oaker said, "Now I want to pass the wishing rod around, and let each of you make one wish." Glider asked, "Can I wish for anything? Will any wish I make come true?" Oaker said, "No. There are rules for using the wishing rod. You are not allowed to wish for anything that isn't possible. If you do, the wishing-helper will tell you that he cannot help you, and that your wish has been denied. You are not allowed to wish for just having to do less work to get something done. If you do, the wishing-helper will tell you that he cannot help you, and that your wish has been denied. And you are not allowed to make a wish that is opposite of another wish. If you do, both wishes will be denied."

Lark asked, "You mean the wishing-helper can't do more than we can do?" Oaker said, "The wishing-helper can do anything he wants to do. If he grants a wish, he can make it happen. He has absolute power.

But if he thinks you're wishing for something that's impossible for you, he'll deny the wish."

Maya asked, "What happens when a wish is denied?" Oaker answered, "Nothing happens. But if you make a wish that is denied, the wishing rod will no longer work for you. If you try to use it afterwards, the wishing-helper won't come when you call." Glider asked, "But can't one always wish for something anyhow?" Oaker answered, "Of course. One can always wish. One just can't use the wishing rod anymore. So if one wants to keep the power of the wishing rod, one must be careful not to use it for any wish that will be denied."

Oaker raised the wishing rod, and said, "Honorable wishing-helper, please come." The wishing-helper stepped out from behind a tree. He stood in front of Oaker, and said, "Dear friend, what is your wish?" Oaker said, "I wish that you stay here until each of my friends has made a wish." The wishing-helper said, "Your wish is granted, dear friend."

Oaker handed the wishing rod to Azalea who sat next to him. She took the rod, and said, "I know I'm supposed to wish only for something that's possible. That is not so easy for me. I never went to college. I'm not as smart as some of you. I never knew much except dancing. Everyone has said it isn't possible for Glider to walk again. Maya and the other doctors in the hospital know about science. They have said it isn't possible. Oaker and Ashly know about magic. They have said it isn't possible. They may be right. It may not be possible. But I don't care. Maybe all of them are wrong. I wish for Glider to walk again."

The wishing-helper said, "Dear friend, you have made an honorable wish. But your wish is not possible. I am sorry that I cannot help you. Your wish is denied."

Azalea handed the wishing rod to Glider who sat next to her. He took the rod, and said, "There is a beggar at the street corner. He says that he cannot get a job because he cannot use his left arm. He has a little boy. I believe the beggar would be able to take better care of his little boy if he had a job. I wish the beggar to have a job." The wishing-helper said, "Dear friend, you have made an honorable wish. Your are right, the beggar is a good man. He really wants to take better care of his little boy. But he has been a beggar for many years. He likes being a beggar. He doesn't want a job. You cannot make him do what he doesn't want to do. Your wish is not possible. I am sorry that I cannot help you. Your wish is denied."

Glider handed the wishing rod to Stari who sat next to him. She took the rod, and said, "When I was young, I couldn't skate. I thought I was stupid. I thought I would never be able to skate. I felt very bad. Then Ashly gave me the forgetting chain. I forgot that I couldn't skate. Streamer taught me to skate. I became his skating partner and his wife. Now I'm very happy. The forgetting chain changed my life. There are many people in the world who think they can't do things. I wish all of them to get forgetting chains, so they'll be as happy as I am."

The wishing-helper said, "Dear friend, you have made an honorable wish. But a forgetting chain is only good for some people. Before Ashly gave you the forgetting chain, you were a very good typist. You could type very fast. You never made mistakes. The forgetting chain didn't teach you to skate. It only helped you forget that you couldn't. You can't help all people with the same magic. Different people need different magic. Your wish is not possible. I am sorry that I cannot help you. Your wish is denied."

Stari handed the wishing rod to Streamer who sat next to her. He took the rod, and said, "I think Stari is wonderful. I like her more than I like anyone else in the world. She likes me too. And she is my skating partner. I wish Stari will always be my skating partner, and will always like me as much as she likes me now." The wishing-helper said, "Dear friend, you have made an honorable wish. It could happen that, as the years pass, Stari will remain your skating partner, and will always like you as much as she likes you now. But one cannot make this happen. People's feelings change. People don't feel the way they do because they want to feel that way. They just do. One must accept this. Your wish is not possible. I am sorry that I cannot help you. Your wish is denied."

Streamer handed the wishing rod to Henna who sat next to him. She took the rod, and said, "When I married Wolf, it was a mistake. He went to another town, and left me alone with my little boy, Flyer. For many years, Flyer was my whole life. He was all I had. I took very good care of him. I helped him in every way I could. Now Flyer is growing up. He wants to be a skater. This is wonderful. He is a very good skater. I am happy that he is. But I see him jump on the ice, and I worry about him all the time. I worry that he will fall and hurt himself. I wish that Flyer will never fall and hurt himself." The wishing-helper said, "Your wish is granted, dear friend."

Henna handed the wishing rod to Mole who sat next to her. He took the rod, and said, "I grew up alone. No one ever took care of me. No one ever liked me. I never thought that anyone would ever like me. All I wanted was to make shoes that fit perfectly. Then I was very lucky. I found Henna. She likes me. I'm very happy. I don't need anything else. I also think it may be unwise to wish for too much. I wish that the next pair of shoes I make will fit perfectly." The wishing-helper said, "Your wish is granted, dear friend."

Mole gave the wishing rod to Flyer who sat next to him. He took the rod, and said, "My mother has always been very good to me. She has taken good care of me. She is a very good mother. But now I need to grow up. I want to become a skater. Glider often says that someday I will be the best skater in the world. If that happens, I will be glad. I will be glad for myself. And I will be glad because it will make Glider happy. But that is not what I wish. I wish to become the best skater I can be. If I fall when I try, then I must fall. If I get hurt when I try, then I must get hurt. I'm very sorry, mother. This is what I must do to grow up." The wishing-helper said, "Dear friend, you have made an honorable wish. Your wish alone is possible. Your mother's wish alone is possible. Together, the two wishes are not possible. I am sorry, Henna. I cannot help you. I am sorry, Flyer. I cannot help you. Both wishes are denied."

Flyer handed the wishing rod to Maya who sat next to him. She took the rod, and said, "Lark is often like a little boy. At such times, he doesn't know the difference between what is possible and what is impossible. I wish that Lark will always wish only for what is possible." The wishing-helper said, "Dear friend, you have made an honorable wish. But Lark is a poet. He dreams a lot. He doesn't always know the difference between what is possible and what isn't. Your wish is not possible. I am sorry that I cannot help you. Your wish is denied."

Maya handed the wishing rod to Lark who sat next to her. He took the rod, and said, "From the time I was a little boy, I always wanted to fly over the mountains like an eagle. Today I understand that I cannot do this. But I wish that someday I will be able to imagine what an eagle feels when he flies high over the mountains." The wishing-helper said, "Your wish is granted, dear friend." Then the wishing-helper stepped away from the table. He stepped behind a tree and was gone.

Oaker said, "Now I will tell you how I got the wishing rod. Many years ago, I was a builder of houses. I drew plans. I hired carpenters, plumbers and electricians to build each house. One day, a man came to see me. He wore blue pants and a blue shirt with gold buttons. He was a wishing-helper, but I didn't know this at the time. He told me about a man by the name of Spruce in another town. He said that Spruce was old and wise. He said that Spruce wanted to build a school for children who didn't have a school. He told me to go and talk to him. I did. I told Spruce it would cost a lot of money to build the school. He said that was all right. I told him I only wanted to build a school that was beautiful. He said he had heard I was a good builder, and that I could build the school any way I thought best. I drew the plans. I hired the workers. We built the school.

"Spruce and I became friends. We talked about many things. I learned many things from him. One day, Spruce invited me to come to a party. It was his pass-along anniversary party. There were ten people at the party. Spruce showed us a stick. He said it was a wishing rod. He asked each of us to make a wish with the wishing rod. I was the only one whose wish was granted by the wishing-helper. Spruce explained that it was his pass-along anniversary. It was exactly twenty-five years since he had gotten the wishing rod. On this day, he had to pass the wishing rod along to someone else. He gave it to me. He said that, exactly twenty-five years from that day, I should give the wishing rod to someone else. That day is today. Only Lark and Mole have made wishes that were granted by the wishing-helper. Now I must choose between them.

"Lark is more likely to make grand wishes. Mole is more likely to make modest wishes. If a wish is too grand, it may be impossible. If it is too modest, it may help too little. I have decided to pass along the wishing rod to Lark and Mole together." Oaker broke the wishing rod into two pieces. He gave one to Lark and one to Mole, and continued, "When the two of you agree on a wish, stand side by side and hold the two pieces of the wishing rod so they touch. Then one of you can call the wishing-helper. The other can tell him your wish. Now, let's make sure you know how to do it. Make your first wish together."

Lark and Mole whispered to each other. They stood side by side. They held the two halves of the wishing rod so they touched. Mole said, "Honorable wishing-helper, please come." The wishing-helper stepped out from behind a tree. He stood before Lark and Mole, and said, "Dear friends, what is your wish?" Lark said, "No meal is complete without dessert. We wish a chocolate cake big enough for all of us."

The wishing-helper said, "Your wish is granted, dear friends." Two assistants came out, carrying a big chocolate cake. The other two assistants brought plates and forks. Everyone got a big piece of cake.

While they were eating the cake, Maya asked Oaker, "In the twenty-five years you've had the wishing rod, did you use it often?" Oaker said, "No, only a few times." Glider asked, "Can you tell me one thing you wished for?" Oaker said, "I wished to find a beautiful place where we could build a cabin. We found this place. Ashly and I have been happy here." Streamer said, "If you didn't use the wishing rod often, then it didn't help you much." Oaker said, "It helped a great deal." Maya asked, "How did it help?" Oaker smiled and said, "Every time we thought of making a wish, we had to think very hard about whether the wish was possible or not. And if we decided the wish was possible, we had to work very hard to make it come true."

11. The Jumping Toothache

One morning, Lark woke up with a toothache. It was a strange toothache. Lark said, "Maya, please look into my mouth. I have a toothache." Maya looked into his mouth, and said, "I don't see anything, but this doesn't mean anything. If your teeth are bothering you, you must go to Driller, the dentist." Lark said, "You know I hate to go to the dentist." Maya said, "Driller is a very good dentist. It's better to go to the dentist than to walk around with a toothache. You know this. So don't put it off. Go right away. Go this morning."

Lark knew that Maya was right. He went to Driller. Driller asked, "Where does it hurt?" Lark said, "I have a strange toothache. First it hurts here." He pointed at a tooth on the right side of his mouth. "Then it hurts here." He pointed at a tooth on the left side of his mouth. "It takes turns. You might say it's a jumping toothache." Driller shook his head, and said, "I will take a look."

Driller put on the big light. He used a metal instrument. He touched all of Lark's teeth. He touched the gums. Then he said, "I don't see any cavities. Your teeth look very good. Your gums look very healthy. If you have a problem, it must be inside your tooth where I can't see it. So we will take x-rays. The dental assistant took the x-rays. After a while, she came back with them. Driller put them up against a plate of glass with light behind it. He shook his head, and said, "Your teeth are perfect. But that's not all." Lark asked, "What else is there?" Driller said, "I've been a dentist for many years. But I've never, absolutely never, heard of a jumping toothache. Your problem must be in your head."

Lark started to say something, but Driller interrupted him, "I'm not saying it doesn't hurt. I'm not saying it isn't important. I'm only saying your problem isn't in your teeth. I think you should see Shrinker, the head doctor. He's very good. I've gone to him myself. He helped me." Lark said, "But I don't have a problem in my head."

Driller said, "I can only tell you there's nothing wrong with your teeth. You say you have a toothache. Not just an ordinary toothache, but a jumping toothache." Driller shook his head and started to laugh, "A jumping toothache. Who ever heard of a jumping toothache?" He laughed some more. He laughed so hard he couldn't go on speaking. Finally, he stopped and said, "If you think you have a jumping toothache, you better go see Shrinker. Take my word for it. That's the smart thing to do."

Lark didn't like the way Driller had talked to him. But he still had the toothache. So he went to see Shrinker. He was surprised to see that Shrinker wore a hat in his office. It was a soft dark blue wool hat like artists used to wear. Lark asked, "Do you always wear this hat?" Shrinker said, "No. This is an indoor hat. I never wear it outside. All right. What's your problem?" Lark said, "I have a strange toothache. It jumps." Shrinker said, "That's interesting." Lark said, "I think, maybe it isn't a real toothache. Maybe it's all in my head. That's why I've come to see you." Shrinker said, "Are you single or married?" Lark said, "I'm married." Shrinker asked, "Do you like your wife?" Lark said, "I like her very much." Shrinker asked, "Does she like you?" Lark said, "She says I am her everything."

Shrinker said, "We will start from the beginning." Lark asked, "From the beginning of my toothache?" Shrinker said, "No. From the beginning of your life. Think back as far as you can. Were you ever afraid of anything?" Lark said, "Yes, when I was small, I was afraid of the dark." Shrinker said, "Aha, I thought so. Were you ever afraid of the dark after you were all grown up?" Lark said, "Yes. Not too long ago." Shrinker said, "Aha, I thought so. We will have to find out why you were afraid of the dark." Lark said, "I know why I was afraid of the dark. I wasn't really afraid of the dark at all. I was really afraid of dying."

Shrinker asked, "What do you think of when you're afraid of dying?" Lark said, "I don't think of anything. I'm no longer afraid of dying." Shrinker said, "Very interesting. Who cured you?" Lark said, "A very wise man. He lives half way up the mountain." Shrinker asked, "How did he cure you?" Lark said, "He cured me with a golden handkerchief." Shrinker said, "Very interesting. Tell me about it."

Lark said, "The golden handkerchief is all black. But when you look closer, you can see golden threads in it. There is a sun in the middle, and there are golden rays in all directions. My wife Maya had to put the golden handkerchief over my face for exactly one minute. When she did, I died. Then I saw that there was nothing to be afraid of. I haven't been afraid of dying since then. I haven't been afraid of the dark since then. I haven't been afraid of anything since then."

Shrinker said, "Very interesting. One makes the patient believe he has died, and the patient is cured." Lark said, "But I really died." Shrinker said, "Of course. The cure wouldn't work if you didn't believe you did. I will have to talk to this mountain doctor of yours sometime. In the meantime, we have to find out what's giving you the jumping toothache. Have you ever been sad?" Lark said, "Yes." Shrinker said, "I mean, not just ordinary sad, but very, very sad." Lark said, "Yes. I was very, very sad. I didn't want to go anywhere. I didn't want to do anything." Shrinker said, "Aha, now we're getting somewhere. We must find out why you were sad."

Lark said, "I know why I was sad." Shrinker said, "Really? Why were you sad?" Lark said, "I was sad because my magic pen didn't write by itself." Shrinker said, "I see. A magic pen? And you say it wrote by itself?" Lark said, "No. I said, it didn't write by itself. That's why I was sad." Shrinker said, "So we must find out why it stopped writing." Lark said, "I know why it stopped writing." Shrinker said, "Really? Why did it stop?" Lark said, "It stopped because the editor of the newspaper wanted me to write only funny poems that rhyme." Shrinker said, "Aha. You're a poet. That explains a lot. You imagine things. That can be a sign of sickness in ordinary people. But it's all right in poets. So you didn't want to write funny poems that rhyme?" Lark said, "That's right. And when I stopped, I was no longer sad."

Shrinker asked, "So what kind of poems do you write now?" Lark said, "Any poems the pen writes." Shrinker said, "Aha, the pen writes again. You have put it together very well. Are you satisfied with the poems you write now?" Lark said, "No. I'm not satisfied."

Shrinker said, "Aha, finally we're getting somewhere. I should have known it would be the poems. What's wrong with the poems you write?" Lark said, "Nothing is wrong with them. They are good poems. When I read them at the Parlor, the people clap." Shrinker said, "But you're not satisfied." Lark said, "Of course, I'm not satisfied. I'm still young. If I were satisfied, I would want to stay where I am. But I want to change. I want to write better poems all the time."

Shrinker said, "Here's the whole picture as I see it. You like your wife. She likes you. You like your work. You were sad once. You're not sad anymore. You were afraid once. You're not afraid anymore. I don't think there's anything wrong with your head. Your mountain doctor has done a very good job. If you have a toothache, go to a dentist. Driller is a good dentist. I use him myself. Go to him." Lark said, "Thank you very much. I'll do that."

When Lark left Shrinker's office, he remembered the wishing rod. He went home. He took his half of the wishing rod, and went to Mole's store. He told Mole about his jumping toothache. He told him that he had gone to Driller and to Shrinker. Then he said, "It's obvious neither of them can help me. I still have the jumping toothache. Do you think we could use the wishing rod to make it go away?"

Mole said, "If you want to make this wish, I'll make it with you. But I think this might be a mistake." Lark asked, "Why a mistake? Why do we keep the wishing rod if we aren't going to use it?" Mole said, "The wishing rod will help only if the wish is possible. Driller couldn't fix your toothache. Shrinker couldn't fix your toothache. Maybe it can't be fixed. Perhaps we could make a smaller wish?" Lark asked, "What smaller wish?" Mole said, "Perhaps we could just wish to find out where the jumping toothache comes from." Lark said, "Mole, I'm happy that you're my wishing partner." Mole said, "Thank you. I'm happy too."

They stood side by side. Their halves of the wishing rod touched. Then Lark said, "Honorable wishing-helper, please come." Immediately, the door of Mole's store opened and the wishing-helper came in. He said, "Dear friends, what is your wish?" Mole said, "Lark has a jumping toothache. We wish to know where this toothache comes from."

The wishing-helper said, "Your wish is granted, dear friends. The jumping toothache comes from magic. It comes from mean magic. You were very wise that you didn't ask me to cure this toothache. This wish would have been denied. Mean magic is very special. It's magic against a particular person. Right now, it's magic against you, Lark. It is a test. It can be overcome only by you. If you don't overcome it, it will make bigger and bigger jumps, until it will kill you. But if you overcome it, you will be stronger than before. After that, no mean magic will ever be able to hurt you again."

The wishing-helper walked out of the store. Lark wanted to see where he went, but by the time Lark got through the door, the wishing-helper was gone.

Mole asked, "What are you going to do about the mean magic?" Lark said, "I don't know what I'll do. But I believe I'll know what to do when the time comes. In the meantime, I'll go walking by the river. I'll try to think of a new poem. And I'll try to pay no attention to the mean magic."

Lark left Mole's store. He tried to think only about his new poem. There were two bridges over the river. He passed the first bridge and went on. The second bridge was far away. When he came to the second bridge, he was tired. He stopped, and sat down on one of the benches near the bridge. He leaned back and closed his eyes for a moment. When he opened them, he saw that someone was sitting next to him. It was Featherman.

Lark said, "What are you doing here?" Featherman said, "What do you mean, what am I doing here? I'm doing the same thing you are doing here. I'm resting from my walk." Lark said, "There are many benches along this path. Did you have to sit on this particular bench?" Featherman said, "What's wrong with this particular bench? It's a fine bench. Why shouldn't I sit here? It's a public bench, isn't it? Why are you so rude? Why aren't you more grateful? I gave you a first prize, a precious count-down watch. What did you do with it? You lost it. That was terrible. To lose such a valuable prize. Then I gave you a second prize, a ruby ring. I see you're not wearing it. I'm afraid to ask what you did with it. I bet, you'll tell me you lost it too." Lark said, "No. I didn't lose it. I gave it away."

Featherman cried out, "Oh, no, no, no. That's even worse. If you had just lost it, that would have been carelessness. But giving it away was stupidity. That's terrible. And here I've been thinking of giving you the third prize. Well, you know how much I like you. I'll forgive you once more. I'll give you the prize anyhow. But this is your last chance. There are only three prizes." Lark said, "Maybe I don't want your prize." Featherman said, "Why do you always say these foolish things. You should really know better by now. Of course, you want the prize. You wanted each prize I gave you, didn't you? You paid me a dollar each time, didn't you? I made you pay the dollar each time, so you couldn't say later on that you didn't want the prize. Stop wasting my time. The third prize is the best of all. It's the last prize. There are no other prizes after that. You are very lucky. The third prize is the golden handkerchief."

Featherman spread out the golden handkerchief in front of Lark. Lark knew that when one covered one's face with it, one died. That's why Oaker had been so careful to make Mole use the stopwatch. But Lark didn't say anything. He just asked Featherman, "So what's this hand-kerchief for?" Featherman said, "If you ever have a pain of some kind." Lark interrupted, and asked, "What kind of pain?" Featherman said, "It doesn't matter what kind of pain. Any kind. A headache, an earache, a stomach ache, a toothache, any kind of pain. As I was saying, if you ever have a pain of some kind, just go to a quiet place. Put the golden hand-kerchief over your face, and the pain will go away. You'll never have that pain again. Now give me a dollar so I can go."

Lark jumped up from the bench, and turned toward Featherman.. Featherman cried out, "What are you doing?" Lark came closer, and said, "I want to give you a hug to thank you." Featherman stepped back. He stretched out both arms in front of him to keep Lark away, and hissed, "Why do you want to thank me suddenly? You never thanked me before. You can't hug me. Just give me a dollar." Lark said, "This time, Feather-man, I won't give you a dollar. I don't want your prize." Featherman said, "If you don't have a pain right now, you don't have to use the handker-chief right now. You can save it, just in case."

For a moment, Lark thought, "I wouldn't have to use the golden handkerchief. Here's my chance to get one. I could save it, just like Oaker did." Then he thought, "But Oaker is wise enough to know how to use it. I'm not wise enough for that. I might use it badly." And he said to Featherman, "I don't want to use the golden handkerchief, Feather-man. And I don't want to save it. But I thank you, Featherman. You were right. It's all just like you said. You've always helped me. When you gave me the first prize, I was very foolish. But I was protected by good people. When you gave me the second prize, I was a little smarter, but not smart enough. I still gave you the dollar. Now I know a little more. I don't want the third prize. I don't want any prize from you. Thank you, Feather-man." Featherman cried out, "You're impossible. You ruin everything. I'm not going to waste my time with you anymore. I'm through with you. Finished. Done with. You've lost your chance. Goodbye." Feath-erman jumped under the bridge. Lark ran after him to look under the bridge, but no one was there. Featherman was gone

Lark started to walk back home. The jumping toothache was gone. Lark thought about the three prizes. Maya had thrown away the first one. Mole had thrown away the second one. Now he had refused the third one. He had finally passed the test. He would never have to deal with Featherman again.

12. The Indoor Hat

Oaker needed new shoes. He came to town and went to Mole's store. After Mole measured Oaker's feet, Oaker asked about Lark. Mole said Lark had a jumping toothache. A dentist told him there was nothing wrong with his teeth. A head-doctor told him there was nothing wrong with his head. Oaker said, "That's strange. It doesn't happen often that a head-doctor tells you there's nothing wrong with your head. I want to talk to Lark." Mole said, "Lark always goes down to the river. That's where he thinks about the next poem he wants to write."

Oaker went to the river. He met Lark and said, "I'm curious about your head-doctor. I'd like to meet him." Lark said, "That's funny. He said the same thing." Oaker asked, "When?" Lark said, "He asked many questions. I think that's what head-doctors do. I told him about the golden handkerchief. I think he didn't believe me. I think he believed I didn't really die. But he said he wanted to meet you. I told him you live halfway up the mountain. Then he called you the mountain doctor." Oaker smiled, and said, "That's all right. I'll call him the valley doctor. Where is he?" Lark said, "I'll take you to his office."

As they turned into the street where Shrinker's office was, Oaker said, "Do you see this man there? Doesn't he look funny?" It was Shrinker. Shrinker said, "Hello, Lark. This must be your mountain doctor." Lark said, "That's right." Oaker said, "And this funny looking man must be your valley doctor." Lark said, "That's right." Oaker turned to Shrinker and said, "So you're the one who told Lark there's nothing wrong with his head?" Shrinker answered, "That's right. And you're the one who cured Lark with a handkerchief?" Oaker said, "That's right." Lark didn't understand what was happening.

Suddenly both Oaker and Shrinker began to laugh. Their bodies shook with laughter. They laughed so hard people stopped to look at them. Then they gave each other a big hug. Oaker said, "The moment I heard of a head-doctor who told Lark there's nothing wrong with his head, I knew it was you." And Shrinker said, "The moment Lark spoke about a golden handkerchief, I knew it was you. So you still have the handkerchief?" Oaker said, "That's right. And you still have the indoor hat?" Shrinker said, "That's right. And how about the wishing rod?" Oaker said, "No. I passed my anniversary." Shrinker exclaimed, "Twenty-five years already? It seems like yesterday. But let's not stand here in the street. Come on up to my office. It's right in the next building."

They went up to Shrinker's office, and sat down. Lark said, "So the two of you have known each other all along." Both laughed. Then Shrinker said, "We were friends in the oval circle. But after our teacher died, the circle fell apart. We all went our different ways. We still met sometimes, but not often. The last time I saw you, Oaker, was just after you got the wishing rod. Then you went on to build more and more houses, didn't you?" Oaker said, "That's right. And you went on working as a head-doctor. Didn't you? And you're still using your indoor hat." Shrinker said, "Absolutely. There it is."

Lark turned. The blue hat was right on top of Shrinker's desk. He asked, "What's an indoor hat?" Shrinker said, "When you're wearing the indoor hat, you feel what the person you're with is feeling." Lark asked, "You mean you can read their mind?" Shrinker said, "No. It isn't that way. You don't know exactly what they are thinking. But in a way you do. Because you know what they are feeling. Here, try it on."

Shrinker put the hat on Lark's head, and said, "Look at me. What do you see?" Lark said, "I see a lake in a park in a city. The water of the lake is calm. The lake is quiet. But the city outside is noisy. The noises are far away and faint, but I can hear them." Oaker said, "Shrinker is calm himself. But he's connected to the people who come to him. You can hear them from a distance."

Shrinker said, "Now look at Oaker. What do you see?" Lark said, "I see a deep lake. The water is clear. There are high mountains all around the lake. They protect the lake." Shrinker said, "Oaker is calm. His calm can't be disturbed. Not even in a storm."

Lark asked, "And why is it called the indoor hat?" Shrinker said, "Because you wear it indoors, with only one or two people nearby. You can't wear it around a lot of people. Actually, you can, but it's very unpleasant. It can even be dangerous. I see you're curious about the hat. Borrow it. Take it with you for an hour. This'll give the two of us a chance to talk about old times. Use it indoors. If you want to try it outside, try it only for a very short time. One minute. On your watch. I don't mean approximately one minute. I mean absolutely no longer than one minute. All right?"

Lark took off the hat, and said, "I'll be back in an hour." He was going to Mole's store. The street was busy. Many people were there. Lark checked his watch. He put on the hat. Immediately, he was in a hurricane. The wind howled. It hurt his ears. Huge waves crashed down on houses. People were swept away, drowning. There were screams all around. It was only three quarters of a minute, but he had enough. He took off the hat. It was like Shrinker had said. The hat was not for where a lot of people were rushing around.

When Lark got to Mole's store, he made sure he closed the door behind him before he put the hat on again. As usual, Mole got up from his work bench as soon as Lark came into the store. He asked, "What's new with the toothache?" Lark said, "It's like I told you. The toothache is gone. The mean magic is over." Mole said, "I'm glad." Lark looked at Mole. He saw a wide river with a huge rock in the middle. The river flowed quietly around the rock.

The door opened. A woman came into the store. It was Lila, the newspaper reporter. She said to Mole, "Are you the shoemaker?" Lark said, "Hello. Do you remember me? I'm Lark." Lila said, "Yes. I remember you. Hello." Then she turned back to Mole, and said, "I need a pair of shoes." Lark looked at Lila. He saw a round stone pool in a fancy garden. There were fountains around the rim of the pool, and there was a fountain in the middle. The water in the middle fountain rose higher than the water in the other fountains.

Mole said, "I will measure your feet and will make you shoes that fit perfectly." Lila said, "Very good. When will the shoes be ready?" Mole said, "You can pick them up one week from today." Lila cried out, "No, no, no. That's impossible. I'm going on a very important trip out of town. It's for the newspaper. I must have the shoes by the day after tomorrow."

Mole said, "I'm sorry. That's impossible." Lila said, "What do you mean, impossible? This trip is for the newspaper. The newspaper will pay you extra to make the shoes fast." Mole said, "What they pay has nothing to do with it. I can't make shoes that fit perfectly in two days." Lila said, "Then make shoes that don't fit perfectly. I must have them."

Mole said, "I don't make shoes that don't fit perfectly." Lila said, "This is ridiculous. I am the customer. I don't care whether the shoes fit perfectly. I'll take them even if they don't. I'll pay the full price even if they don't." Lark looked at Mole. The river had become narrow. It had stopped flowing. The rock blocked the water completely. There was nothing but rock. Mole said, "I don't care that you're the customer. I don't care that you'll take the shoes anyhow. I don't care that you'll pay for them. I only make shoes that fit perfectly."

Lila said, "You're a selfish, stubborn man, full of vanity." Lark asked Lila, "Why are you so angry?" Lila said, "I'm angry because this shoemaker doesn't want to do what I tell him to do." Lark looked at Lila. The fountains around the rim were no longer working. The fountain in the middle was shooting water high into the air. Lark said, "Perhaps you say hurtful things because you want to be more important than other people." Lila said, "I just tell it the way it is. One must always tell the truth." Lark said, "If the truth hurts people, it may be better to say nothing, or perhaps even something that isn't true. Be patient for a while. Let me talk to Mole."

Lark put his arm around Mole, and led him to the side of the room where Lila couldn't hear them. Then he said to Mole, "I know you want to make only shoes that fit perfectly. I think this is wonderful. But there are good reasons and bad reasons for anything. There was a time when you thought people would like you more if you made shoes that fit perfectly. You found out this wasn't so. Now you want to make shoes that fit perfectly, just to make shoes that fit perfectly. That would be good if it were true. But it isn't." Mole said, "What do you mean, it isn't?" Lark said, "I think you're afraid something terrible will happen if you make shoes that don't fit perfectly. But nothing terrible will happen. I think this is a good time to make shoes that don't fit perfectly. Just once." Mole thought for a while. Then he said, "I don't want to. I can't."

Lark reached into his pocket. He took out a coin and showed it to Mole. He said, "This is a magic coin. Do you remember Glider's birthday party? You gave him a magic coin. I'm giving it back to you now." Mole said, "But it's not the same coin." Lark said, "That's right. The coin you gave Glider was the coin you got the first time you made shoes that fit perfectly. This coin is for the first time since then that you're going to make shoes that don't fit perfectly. Just put it with your tools, and make the shoes."

Mole took the coin. He turned back to Lila, and said, "All right. Let me measure your feet. I'll make your shoes. You can pick them up the day after tomorrow." Lila said, "Thank you, Mole. I really need the shoes."

After she left, Lark looked at Mole. The river was a little wider. It was flowing again. Lark took off the indoor hat, and said to Mole, "I'll be here the day after tomorrow. I want to know what happens with Lila's shoes."

Lark walked back to Shrinker's office. He arrived a few minutes before the hour was up. Oaker and Shrinker were still talking. Lark gave the hat back to Shrinker, and asked, "Does every head-doctor have an indoor hat?" Shrinker said, "No. Very few have an indoor hat." Lark asked, "Did you have the indoor hat before you went to school to become a head-doctor?" Shrinker said, "Yes. I've had the indoor hat for a very long time." Lark asked, "Then why did you go to school to become a head-doctor? Why didn't you just use your indoor hat to help people?" Shrinker smiled and said, "I could have done that. But then no one would have been willing to pay me. Do you see? That's how it is."

Two days later, Lark went back to Mole's store. Mole said, "I made the shoes for Lila. They didn't fit perfectly. But Lila was happy. I will go on making shoes that fit perfectly. They'll fit perfectly almost all of the time. Thank you, Lark for your magic coin. I'm finally free. From now on, the shoes I make will fit perfectly, not because I have to make them that way, but because I want to make them that way."

Lark didn't have the indoor hat anymore. But he could still see the rock in the river. The rock was as big as it had ever been. But the river was much wider than ever before. It flowed calmly around the rock.

13. The Squeezing Egg

Leada and Seeker were twins. Their father, Fuller, was the owner of the Fuller furniture company. Their mother, Mora, was dead. Mora had been a woman with strong opinions. She had wanted her children to accomplish things she had not accomplished herself. She had wanted Leada to become a doctor. She had wanted Seeker to become a lawyer. Leada had gone away to study to become a doctor. But Seeker wanted to become a philosopher. Mora hadn't thought this was a good idea. She had said, "Someone always needs a doctor. Someone always needs a lawyer. But no one ever needs a philosopher."

Seeker had asked his father to help. Fuller had talked to Mora. He had said, "I think Leada and Seeker should decide for themselves what kind of work they'll do. That way, they won't be able to blame their mother. They won't be able to blame their father. And if they make a mistake, they'll learn from it." Mora had not been convinced, but she had agreed.

Now, Seeker was back, and Fuller asked him how his studies were going. Seeker said, "They are going wonderfully well. I'm learning new things all the time. I'm learning about all the different things that people have figured out about the world for three thousand years. I'm learning what they've figured out about the meaning of life. That's very exciting."

Fuller asked, "What have they figured out?" Seeker replied, "That's just it. In all those years, all those smart people haven't figured out anything at all." Fuller asked, "And that's exciting?" Seeker said, "Yes. Because I have. That's what's exciting. I've been thinking about it for a long time. Ever since I was sixteen years old. I started to write it down three years ago. I'm almost finished. It'll take maybe six more months. People will be so surprised. They'll say, isn't it wonderful that someone has figured it out finally."

Fuller said, "Maybe people won't think what you've figured out is so wonderful." Seeker said, "Yes, they will. Perhaps they won't understand it right away. Perhaps it'll take a long time. But in the end, they will. And when they do, I'll be famous. That's wonderful. It's all wonderful, except for the waiting." Fuller asked, "What's so terrible about waiting?"

Seeker said, "Waiting is terrible. It upsets me that I have the answer, and no one knows it. It upsets me that I have to wait for people to find out. I wish I could hurry it up." Fuller asked, "Are you sure that's what you want?" Seeker said, "Yes. I think about it all the time. I wish the time when everyone knows what I've figured out were here already."

Fuller said, "If that's really what you want, then perhaps I can help you." Seeker cried out, "How? It's impossible." Fuller answered, "I said perhaps. Perhaps it's impossible. And perhaps it's possible. I don't know. But if you want, we can try to find out." Seeker said, "Of course, I want."

Fuller left the room. He came back, carrying an egg. He said, "Get a few people together. Tell them you want to hike up Hatchet mountain. If you start early Saturday, you can get to the top before evening. Take a tent and sleeping bags. Stay on top of the mountain over night. Come down Sunday. Take this. It's a squeezing egg. Put it in a safe place in your room. When you're ready to leave Saturday morning, squeeze it hard, and put it in your pocket." Seeker asked, "Won't it break?" Fuller said, "No. It's a squeezing egg. It won't break. Once you put it in your pocket, don't touch it again. Keep it in your pocket for the entire hike. Keep it in your pocket when you sleep at night. Take it out only after you get to the river on your return. Put it in your backpack, and come home. We'll talk about it then."

Seeker said, "This sounds strange to me. It's hard to believe the egg won't break when I squeeze it. I guess, I'll see. It's hard to believe it won't break in my pocket during the night. I guess, I'll see. Mostly, it's hard to believe that the egg has anything to do with anything. I guess, I'll see. I know one thing about you, dad. You understand more than one might think, seeing you're only a businessman. Are you sure you're not a philosopher?"

Fuller smiled, and said, "I'm definitely not a philosopher." Seeker said, "Maybe you just don't want to admit it." Fuller said, "No. Philosophers try to figure out how the world is made by thinking about it. I only try to keep in mind some of the things that can't be figured out."

Some of Seeker's friends from the time when he was small worked in the office of the furniture company. Seeker went there and asked whether anyone wanted to go on a hike to the top of Hatchet mountain. Stari said, "If my husband, Streamer, wants to go, I'll go." Stari's friend, Lily, said, "If Stari and Streamer go, I'll go." Next, Seeker went to the factory of the furniture company. The factory was in a different place than the office. Seeker knew Shaper, the manager of the factory. Seeker told Shaper that Lily was going. Shaper said, "If Lily goes, I'll go."

On Saturday, Seeker got up early. He dressed. Then he squeezed the egg hard. The egg didn't break. He put it into his pants pocket. He put on his backpack with food, clothes, a small tent, and a sleeping bag. Then he went to the river. The group met at the first bridge at six o'clock in the morning. There were five of them: Seeker, Shaper, Streamer and Stari, and Lily.

They started to climb. They got to the top of the mountain. It seemed to Seeker that they got there very fast. They made a tent. They woke up next morning. They started down again. They got back to the river. It seemed to Seeker that they got back very fast. Seeker took the egg out of his pants pocket. He put it into his backpack. Now he noticed that he was tired. He noticed that the others were all talking happily.

Stari said, "The first part of the steep road was the hardest." Lily said, "Yes, and it was harder going downhill than uphill." Streamer said, "It's more dangerous going downhill. There's a greater chance of falling. I never heard of anyone falling while going uphill." Shaper said, "The town looked so small from the halfway point." Lily said, "I was wondering whether we would still see it from the top."

Shaper asked, "Which part of the hike did you like best?" Streamer said, "When we came out of the forest, we were suddenly on the meadow. The sun was bright. The colors were clear. The little purple flowers were everywhere. That was beautiful." Stari said, "I liked the views. But I liked the climbing best of all. The steeper it got, the better I liked it. Going up those big rocks was the most wonderful part of all."

Lily said, "I liked the climbing. I liked the meadow in the sun. I liked the view from the top. But the thing I liked most was when the stars came out at night. When we looked up at them, they filled the whole world."

Shaper said, "And the food. Didn't it taste wonderful?" Streamer said, "It was just bread, cheese, tomatoes, and olives. But it was the best meal I ever had." They all agreed. Yes, they said, it tasted so good. It must have been the air. It must have been that we were tired. It must have been that we were hungry.

Streamer turned to Seeker and asked, "And how about you? The hike was your idea. What did you like best?" Seeker said, "I'm not sure. It was a strange hike for me. All I know is, we went up, we came down, and we're back again. I don't remember much else. I guess, I wasn't paying attention. I must have had other things on my mind."

They were walking on the path along the river. Lily asked Seeker, "What kind of person is your father?" Seeker asked, "Don't you know him? You work in the office." Lily said, "True. But I'm only a typist. I've never talked with him. I just see him when he walks by on the way to his office. He always looks like he's thinking about something." Seeker said, "He's full of surprises. You never know what he'll do next." Shaper said, "He comes to the factory. When he finds a mistake, we have to do it over. But I've never seen him angry. We all try hard. We all want to please him."

When Seeker came home, Fuller and he sat down at the large wooden dining room table. Seeker took the egg out of his backpack. He put it on the table. He said, "All right. Here's the egg. I've done what you asked me to do. What now?" Fuller asked, "How was your hike?" Seeker said, "The others thought it was great. But I didn't think much of it. I don't know why they made such a fuss. We went up. We went down. One, two, three, and it was over. The time just passed. It seemed like no time to me." Fuller said, "That's right. I couldn't have said it better myself." Seeker asked, "What do you mean?"

Fuller said, "It seemed like no time to you, because it was no time. Squeezing the egg, speeds up time. The harder one squeezes, the more it speeds it up. After one puts the egg down, time gets back to its regular speed. When we talked last, you said, waiting is terrible. You said it'll take a long time for people to know what you've figured out. You said, you wanted to hurry it up. Here's your chance. Take the egg. Squeeze it real hard. The years will go by in no time. Next thing you know, you'll be there. Here's the egg."

Seeker asked, "You mean I could speed up time and have the book, and everything, and be there?" Fuller said, "That's right. Just like the hike up the mountain." Seeker said, "But I never really went on the hike. I know we went up. I know we came down. But I saw nothing. I felt nothing. It went by so fast, I might as well not have gone at all." Fuller said, "That's how it is. Whether that's a good thing or a bad thing depends on what you really want." Seeker cried out, "What do you mean?"

Fuller said, "If you really want what's at the end, you can squeeze the egg, and be there, as you say, in no time. But you won't know how you got there. If you stop thinking about what's at the end, and just pay attention to everything you see, and hear, and feel on the way, you won't want to speed up time. You'll want to let it pass slowly. You'll want to know and feel every moment. It's up to you. Here's the egg." Seeker pushed the egg back to Fuller, and said, "I don't want it." Fuller asked, "Are you sure?" Seeker said, "I'm absolutely sure."

Fuller brought his flat hand hard down on the egg. The egg broke. The shells, the egg white, and the yoke splattered on the table. Beava, Fuller's housekeeper, came in with a rag and a dust pan. She cleared the mess from the table. She wiped the table clear. The egg was gone. Not a speck was left.

14. The Blink of an Eye

Lila was a newspaper reporter. She was going on a trip for her newspaper. She was going to write a story about a big fire. Large trees, more than one hundred years old, were burning in the forest. She was going to write about the firemen who were trying to put out the fire. Before she left, she went to Mole's store to get new shoes for her trip. There wasn't enough time for Mole to make shoes that fit perfectly. But he made shoes for her anyhow. He made them in just two days.

Lila went on an airplane. Then she went by car to the place where the big fire was. No one was allowed to go in. But Lila was wearing a chain around her neck. There was a tag on the chain. It said "Press" in big letters. This showed that Lila worked for a newspaper.

Lila said to the firemen who stood where the road was closed, "I need to go in with one of your firemen to see what he does." Two firemen came along. They wore helmets. They wore big metal cans on their backs. They held long tubes. They were going to spray chemicals to keep the fire from spreading. One of them heard Lila. He said, "My name is Squasher. I'll take you along. But you must put on a helmet."

Lila got a helmet. She went with Squasher and his partner. They walked through a meadow until they came to the fire. Large old trees were burning. Lila looked up. The wall of fire was bigger than a house. A road led into the forest. It looked like it led right into the fire, but the road was wide enough for the firemen to go in to spray. Lila could feel the heat of the fire. Squasher asked, "Do you want to come in with us to watch us work?" Lila said, "No. I'll wait for you here."

Lila waited. She looked at the meadow in the direction from which they had come. There were no trees there, but the wind shifted. There were some leaves on the meadow. The leaves began to burn. Lila was frightened. Squasher and his partner returned. Squasher said, "All right. We'll go back now." Lila said, "How will we go back? There's fire on the meadow." Squasher laughed and said, "That's nothing. These are very small fires. Just a few leaves close to the ground. You have good shoes. We can walk across the meadow. It's perfectly safe. We do it all the time."

Lila said, "I'm afraid I'll get burned." Squasher said, "We can't stand here all day. If you want, I'll walk ahead of you. I'll walk very slowly. My weight will put out the flames. If you follow in my footsteps, you'll be on solid ground all the way." Lila said, "All right." When they were safely on the other side, she said, "That was a lot of fun. Thank you for taking me. I have a good story for my newspaper."

Lila wrote the story on the plane. She got to the newspaper late in the day. Haggler, the editor of the newspaper, was still there. He read her story. He read it very fast. Editors can read a whole page in just a few moments. Then he said, "This is a good story. We will put it into the newspaper. We will use the headline, 'Giant Trees Burning in Forest'. There's one more thing. The fire is far away. Let's put some human interest into the story, something about our town."

Lila ran to Mole's store. She got there just as he was ready to go home. She said, "Hello, Mole. I'm glad I found you. You made good shoes for me. Now I'll do something for you. I'll put you into my story for the newspaper." Mole said, "I'm not sure I want to be in a story." Lila said, "Yes, you do. If you're in a story, you'll get more customers. I'll be here first thing in the morning with a photographer."

Mole went home and talked with Henna. She said, "I don't know whether being in a story would be a good thing or a bad thing." Mole said, "It might bring more customers." Henna asked, "Do you want more customers?" Mole said, "I usually say, I don't care. But maybe this isn't true." Henna said, "Lark is a good friend. Go talk to Lark. See what he thinks."

Mole went to see Lark. He told him that Lila wanted to put a story about him into the newspaper. Lark asked, "What kind of a story?" Mole said, "I don't know." Lark spoke slowly, "Oaker always says things can be done for a good reason or for a bad reason. I've tried to learn from him. Sometimes I say things I heard him say. I also use my own experience. There was a time when I wanted to have my picture in the newspaper, so people would pay more attention to me. This was not a good reason. It didn't have a good result. I think Oaker would ask why you would want to be in a story." Mole said, "When I was alone, I wanted more attention. Now that Henna and Flyer live with me, I'm happy. But I think it might be good to have more customers." Lark asked, "Why?" Mole said, "I want more money. I want to buy new skates for Flyer. I want to buy him a new skating outfit. I want to buy a new dress for Henna."

Lark said, "This may be a good reason. But it may not be that simple. The decision about the newspaper story may be much more important than it seems. Of course only you can make the decision. But in my opinion, it's not good to have too many customers." Mole thought he heard a click from the front door. He turned around to look at the door. He stared at the door. He saw nothing there, only the door. He turned back to Lark and said, "Thank you for your advice, Lark. I'll try to remember."

Next morning, Lila was there with two photographers. They carried equipment. Lila said to Mole, "You must tell me all about yourself. In the meantime, my assistants will take pictures inside the store. How did you become a shoemaker? When did you find out that you wanted to be a shoemaker?" Mole said, "My parents died when I was young. I didn't have any money to go to school. I lived with people who had a shoe store. I had to work to pay for my food. I worked in their store. I swept the floor. I carried packages. I delivered shoes. I watched the shoemaker. I began to help him. Then I became a shoemaker. That's all." Lila said, "And you try to make shoes that fit perfectly." Mole said, "I don't just try. I make shoes that fit perfectly." Lila said, "Very good." She turned to the photographers and asked, "Did you get the pictures?" One of them said, "Just like you told us." Lila said, "Very good. That's all we need, Mole. Thank you. Goodbye." They packed up and were gone.

When Mole came to the store next morning, five people were waiting outside. They all wanted shoes. Mole measured their feet in turn. He told the first one, "You can pick up your shoes one week from today." He told the next one to pick up the shoes in eight days, the next one in nine days, the next one in ten days. Just when he was finishing with the last one, Henna came into the store. She carried a newspaper.

Two stories were on the front page. The first story had the headline, "Giant Trees Burn in Forest," by Lila, our own reporter who was there and saw it with her own eyes. The second story had the headline, "The Shoes that Saved my Life." Underneath was a picture of the shoes Mole had made for Lila and a picture of the inside of his store. The story described Lila's trip. It went on: "I wanted to get close to the fire. I got so close the heat singed my hair. Then the wind shifted. Suddenly, there was fire all around me. I thought this was the end of my life. I thought I would burn to death. There was only one way out, right through the fire. I had no other choice. I ran through it. My shoes saved my life. These shoes were made right here in our own town, by our own master-shoemaker, Mole."

Then there was a box with the heading "About Mole". It said "From the time Mole was a child, he dreamt of becoming a shoemaker. He dreamt of making shoes that would fit perfectly. After years of study, he invented a method for doing this. All the shoes Mole makes fit perfectly."

Lark came to the store a little later. He asked, "Did you use special leather for Lila's shoes?" Mole said, "No. I'm amazed she was able to go through the fire." Lark said, "Perhaps it wasn't such a big fire."

All day long, people came into Mole's store. They wanted Mole to make shoes for them. Mole told them they might have to wait four or five weeks. They said they would wait. Then Mole told people he would have to put them on a waiting list. At the end of the day, he had a long list.

Just when he was closing the store, a very thin man came. He was the thinnest man Mole had ever seen. His face looked like a skull with a bit of thin skin stretched over it. Mole said, "I'm sorry. I can't make any more shoes. I've too much work already." The man said, "I didn't come for shoes. I'm a shoemaker myself. My name is Ferret. I read about you in the newspaper. Please give me a job. I'll work for you. I'll help you make good shoes. I'll help you make shoes your customers will like." Mole said, "But I've never hired anyone to work for me." Ferret said, "This is a good time to start."

Mole said, "I only make shoes that fit perfectly." Ferret said, "I'll work right next to you. You'll watch me. If I do anything you don't like, I'll change it. You'll sell only shoes that fit perfectly. Together, we'll make more shoes and you won't have to disappoint so many people." Mole said, "I'll try it. But remember, I'll look at every pair of shoes. If I don't like what I see, you'll have to do it over." Ferret was a good shoemaker. Mole liked his work. Mole looked at every pair of shoes Ferret made. There was never anything wrong with them. Mole was happy that he had hired Ferret.

After a few weeks, Ferret said to Mole, "We have too much work for just the two of us. We need two assistants." Mole said, "I don't want to spend time watching assistants." Ferret said, "You won't have to watch them. I'll watch them. I'll watch them very carefully. You'll still look at every pair of shoes before we give it to a customer." Mole said, "All right. But remember, all shoes must fit perfectly." Ferret said, "Absolutely."

The people who got shoes from Mole's store told their friends. More and more people wanted shoes from Mole's store. After a few weeks, Ferret said to Mole, "We need five more assistants." Mole cried out, "Five more assistants? Impossible. Where are we going to put them?" Ferret said, "There's a big building on the next street. It was an ice-house once. It's been empty for many years. I've spoken to the owner. He'll let us have a large room for not much rent. There will be an office for me, and room for twenty assistants." Mole cried out, "Twenty assistants?" Ferret said, "I know we don't need twenty assistants. We need only seven. But we'll have space for more assistants, in case we ever need more."

Mole said, "How will I check the shoes you make at the ice-house?" Ferret said, "Every afternoon, you'll leave the store an hour early. You'll walk over to the ice-house. It isn't a long walk. It won't take you more than five minutes. We'll arrange all the new shoes on one long shelf. You'll be able to look at all the shoes finished that day. I promise you, they'll all fit perfectly." Mole said, "I guess we have to try it."

Ferret rented the room in the ice-house. He got work benches. He promoted two of the assistants to be supervisors. He put a big sign over the door of the ice-house. It said, "Mole Shoe Works. Only shoes that fit perfectly." Henna got a job in the store. She wrote down the names of the customers who wanted shoes. She collected the money. Then she sent them to the ice-house to have their feet measured. Mole still made shoes for some customers, but he had to leave the store right after lunch because there were so many shoes to be looked at to make sure they were made right.

After another month, Ferret rented more space in the ice-house. The Mole Shoe Works had fifty workers. Mole had to leave the store before lunch. Then Ferret said to Mole, "The business is growing. We are very successful. You're spending too much time walking back and forth between the store and the ice-house. I think you should give up the store, and move to the ice-house. You'll have two private rooms next to each other. One room will be your work room. You'll have a new workbench and all the tools you need. You'll be able to make shoes whenever you want. Right next to this room, you'll have an office with a big desk. That's where you'll see important people. You'll be able to walk right out of your office into your work room. You'll be able to walk right out of your office into the factory. You'll be able to see everything, and to make sure everything's done right."

Mole didn't like the idea, but he wanted to be where the shoes were being made. He felt bad about giving up the store, but he gave it up. He moved to the ice-house. The store became a bakery.

At the ice-house, it was like Ferret had said. Mole had a bigger work room. He had a big office next to his work room. But Mole didn't have much time for making shoes. He had meetings all day long. At first, he still looked at every pair of shoes that was finished. But when the number of workers reached two hundred, he couldn't look at all the shoes anymore. He appointed three shoemakers to look at the shoes for him, to make sure they would fit perfectly.

When Mole had the store, Lark came often. They talked about many things. But after Mole moved to the ice-house, Lark didn't come often. Mole worked late every evening. He didn't have time to visit Lark and Maya. So Mole and Lark didn't see each other often anymore.

One day, Mole's secretary said, "There was a man here today. He wanted to see you." Mole asked, "What was his name?" The secretary said, "Lark." Mole cried out, "Why didn't you tell me?" The secretary said, "You were in meetings. I didn't want to disturb you. And the man didn't look very important." Mole asked, "What happened?" The secretary said, "He sat here for a while. Then he started to walk back and forth. He looked like he was thinking about something. Then he said, 'Tell Mole, I was here. I'll come back some other time.' And he left."

Mole felt very bad. He went directly home. Henna was still at the factory. He took his half of the wishing rod and went to Lark's house. He wondered whether Lark would be mad at him. Lark didn't seem to be mad. He wondered whether Lark would be happy to see him. Lark seemed happy to see him. He wanted to talk with Lark. He wanted to explain everything. But he didn't. He said, "Lark, I want you to do something for me." Lark asked, "What?" Mole said, "I want us to make a wish." Lark asked, "What wish?"

Mole said, "We must be careful to wish only for what is possible. I have made big mistakes. I don't think it's possible to change those. But maybe I could make a small wish. Maybe I could wish that I'll always have time to make shoes and see my friends." Lark said, "I'll help you make any wish you want, but I think we could make a bigger wish." Mole liked the idea.

Lark went into the other room. He came back with his half of the wishing rod. They stood next to each other. They touched their halves of their wishing rods. They said, "Honorable wishing-helper, please come." Immediately, the front door opened and the wishing-helper came in. He stood in front of Mole and Lark, and said, "Dear friends, what is your wish?" Mole and Lark said together, "We wish Mole will always have just as many customers as he needs." The wishing helper said, "Your wish is granted, dear friends." He turned and walked to the door. Mole turned around and looked after him. He kept staring at the door until the wishing-helper was gone. He stared until he heard the door click.

Lark said, "I don't know what's the matter with you, Mole. I don't know why you're looking at the door like this. There's nothing there. I don't think you were listening to me. I don't think you heard a word of what I said." Mole said, "I'm sorry Lark. What didn't I hear? What was it you said?" Lark answered, "I said that, in my opinion, it's not good to have too many customers." Mole said, "But I agree with you. I know this. Absolutely. That's why I came. I feel very bad that we haven't seen each other for such a long time." Lark said, "It hasn't been that long." Mole said, "I think it's been very long." Lark said, "But you just saw me yesterday." Mole said, "Yesterday? I don't remember. Where did I see you yesterday?" Lark said, "What's the matter with you, Mole? Don't you remember? I came to your store yesterday." Mole cried out, "Yesterday? To my store? I don't believe it. It's impossible. I must go. I must check."

Mole rushed out of the house. Maya said to Lark, "Go after him and find out what's going on. He's behaving very strangely." Mole was running. Lark was running after him. They passed the ice-house. There was no sign over the door. It was just the empty ice-house. They came to Mole's store. There was no bakery there. It was just Mole's store. Lark caught up with Mole in front of the store. Mole was crying. Between tears, he sobbed, "The store is here. My store is here." Lark said, "What's the matter, Mole? Why are you acting so strangely? Of course, it's here. Where should it be?" Mole said, "I'm happy. I'm very happy."

Mole put his hands in his pocket. His keys were there. He said to Lark, "Go on back home. I'm all right. Really. You don't have to worry about me. But there's something I must do. Thank you for being my friend. Now go home." Lark said, "I guess, you'll be all right. Good night." And he left.

Mole went into the store. He found a sign that said "Closed". He hung the sign in the window. He locked up and went home. Henna asked, "So what did Lark say?" Mole answered, "Lark said it's not a good thing to have too many customers. If anyone asks for me tomorrow morning, tell them I've gone away. Out of town. If they ask when

I'll be back, tell them you don't know. I don't want the people from the newspaper to find me."

Mole stayed in the house all day. The following morning, he asked Henna to bring him the newspaper. There were two stories on the front page. On the left side there was a story with the headline, "Giant Trees Burning in Forest." On the right side was a story with the headline, "A fireman and I walked through the fire together." Mole read the story. Then he went to his store.

Soon after he got to the store, a very thin man came in. It was Ferret. He said, "I'm a shoemaker. I'm looking for a job." Mole said, "I'm sorry. I don't have work for anyone." Ferret said, "I'm a very good shoemaker. Let me prove it to you." Mole said, "I'm sure you're a very good shoemaker, but I make all the shoes myself." Ferret said, "What if you had more work than you could do?" Mole said, "I would send the customers away. I'm sure you're an honest man and a good shoemaker. I'd really like to help you, but I never hire anyone. That's just how it is."

Later in the day, Lark came to the store. He said, "I was worried about you when you ran out of my house so suddenly. Were you upset because you were trying to decide about the newspaper story?" Mole said, "When I ran out of your house, I had already decided." Lark said, "Really? Then you must have decided very fast." Mole answered, "I'm not sure now. It may have taken me a very very long time to decide, or I may have decided in the blink of an eye."

15. The Talking Backpack

Fuller was the owner of the Fuller furniture company. His company made chairs, tables, benches, chests, and other furniture. Everything made by the Fuller furniture company was made to last. If someone bought a chair or a table or anything else from the Fuller furniture company, they knew they would be able to give it to their grandchildren someday.

Fuller had two children, Seeker and Leada. They were twins. They were all grown up. Both were away at school. Seeker wanted to become a philosopher. That is a person who tries to figure out how the world is made just by thinking about it. Leada was studying to be a doctor. She had finished the first two years of her studies. Now she was home for a visit.

Leada was having breakfast with her father. Fuller's chef, Gobbler, who lived in Fuller's house had made a delicious breakfast. Everything Gobbler cooked was delicious. After coffee, Fuller asked, "How do you like studying to be a doctor?" Leada said, "It's all right." Fuller asked, "What part of your studies have you liked most?" Leada said, "There's a lot to memorize. You have to know all the Latin names for the different parts of the body. You also have to know a lot of chemical formulas."

Fuller asked, "Do you like the chemistry?" Leada said, "It doesn't matter. You have to know it. That's all there is to it." Fuller asked, "Are you looking forward to being a doctor?" Leada said, "Mother always wanted me to be a doctor. I knew this from the time I was a little girl. She wanted to become a doctor herself. She was always sorry that she didn't. She didn't want me to make the same mistake. If she were alive now, she would want me to become a doctor."

Fuller said, "I think you should show more respect for your mother." Leada cried out, "What do you mean? What's not respectful?" Fuller said, "Your mother was a very smart woman. We can't be sure what she would say if she were alive. We really don't know. Do we?"

Leada said, "I know my mother. I know exactly what she would say. She would say I should become a doctor. My problem is to decide whether I should become a regular doctor, or perhaps a head doctor. What do you think?" Fuller said, "I can't help you with that. But I know people who may be able to help you. Do you want to talk to them?" Leada said, "Sure. Who should I talk to?"

Fuller said, "I think you should talk to three people. First, Maya. She's a doctor at the hospital. She's a very good doctor. Go see her. Tell her you're my daughter. Tell her you're studying to become a doctor. I'm sure she'll try to help. Then, Shrinker. He's a head doctor. He's a very good head doctor. Go see him. Tell him you're my daughter. You're studying to be a doctor. I'm sure he'll try to help. Then, Shaper. He's not a doctor, but he studied to be a doctor once. Now he's the manager of our factory. The people who make our furniture work for him. Don't tell him you're my daughter. Don't tell him you're studying to be a doctor. Tell him you want to see how our furniture is made. Will you do that?" Leada said, "Sure."

Fuller said, "There's one more thing." He left the room and returned with a small backpack. He gave it to Leada, and said, "This is a talking backpack." Leada looked inside, and said, "There's nothing in it." Fuller said, "That's right. I'd like you to put it on and keep it on. Don't take it off until you're back here." Leada asked, "Are you telling me it'll talk?" Fuller said, "I don't know whether it'll talk. It's called a talking backpack. That's what it's supposed to do. Just keep it on." Leada said, "OK."

Leada went to the hospital to see Maya. It wasn't a very long walk, but she got tired as she walked. When she got there, she asked for Maya. Maya asked, "What is your problem? Does anything hurt?" Leada said, "No. I don't have a problem. Nothing hurts. My name is Leada. I am Fuller's daughter." Maya said, "I know Fuller. He's a very nice man. So why have you come?" Leada said, "I am studying to be a doctor. I've finished the first two years. I'm trying to decide whether I should be a regular doctor, or a head doctor. My father said, I should talk to you and to Shrinker. He also told me to talk to Shaper. He's the manager of the furniture company."

Maya said, "Why don't you take off this backpack while we talk. You'll be more comfortable." Leada said, "Thank you. I really would be more comfortable. But I promised my father I would keep it on all the time. He said, it's not just an ordinary backpack. It's a talking backpack." Maya said, "Really? Has it said anything yet?" Leada said, "Not a word." Maya said, "Don't be too surprised if it never says anything." Leada asked, "So you don't believe in magic?" Maya said, "I believe in science. I've seen some magic with my own eyes. While I see it, I believe it. But when I don't see it anymore, I don't believe it anymore. Anyhow, what would you like to know?"

Leada asked, "How does it feel to be a doctor?" Maya answered, "It's the best thing in the world. Many times sick people come to me, and there's nothing I can do for them. That feels bad. But sometimes, a sick person comes to me, and I make them well. That's wonderful. Don't you think?" Leada said, "I'm not far enough along in my studies yet. When did you know that you wanted to be a doctor?" Maya said, "I knew it right away. I knew it even before I started my studies. I liked every moment. Don't you?" Leada said, "Of course." She felt very tired. She wanted to lie down, but there was nowhere to lie down. She said, "I see people waiting to talk to you. I don't want to take up more of your time. Thank you for talking to me. Now I'm going to see Shrinker." Maya said, "Goodbye and good luck. And let me know if your talking backpack says anything." Leada said, "I'll let you know." When she left, she was so tired she had to sit down on a bench before going on to Shrinker's office.

The moment Shrinker saw her, he said, "Come in, come in. I see you're wearing a talking backpack. Where did you get it?" Leada said, "My father asked me to wear it." Shrinker said, "Really? Who's your father?" Leada said, "Fuller." Shrinker cried out, "Impossible. You are little Leada? Impossible. The last time I saw you," he brought his hand to his knee, "you were so high. How time flies. You were a very pretty little girl. And you've become a very lovely young woman. Fuller must be very proud of you. What brings you here?"

Leada said, "I've been studying to be a doctor. I've finished the first two years. Now I'm trying to decide whether I should become a regular doctor or a head doctor. What do you think?" Shrinker asked, "What does the talking backpack say?" Leada said, "I don't know. It hasn't said a thing. Not one word. And I've been wearing it ever since I left our house this morning. I wouldn't wear it, except I promised my father not to take it off." Shrinker said, "If Fuller said to keep it on, keep it on. One can never know about these things. It might say nothing for a long time, and then suddenly it might talk."

Leada said, "So you believe in magic?" Shrinker said, "Magic is a big word. Anything we can find out by looking and thinking is science. Then there's everything that's left. Different people use different words for it. Some people call it magic. But whatever you call it, there's a lot of it. So it doesn't make much sense to say I believe in it, or I don't believe in it. You see?" Leada said, "All I see is that you didn't answer my question." Shrinker said, "You're a smart young lady. What makes you want to be a head doctor?" Leada said, "I don't know. Should I want to be one?" Shrinker said, "Should you want to be a head doctor? That's a very interesting question. Everyone wants to know what they should want. If you're a head doctor, you listen to people's troubles. Sometimes, very rarely, you help one of them. Just a very little bit. What do you think of that?"

Leada said, "My mother thought that helping people is the most important thing in the world. She thought that's what everyone should try to do." Shrinker said, "There you are. You've answered your own question. What does your father think?" Leada said, "I don't know." Shrinker asked, "Haven't you asked him?" Leada said, "He's funny. He talks around it. He never told me what I should do. He never told me what I should want to do." Shrinker said, "Maybe the talking backpack will tell you. That would be just as good. That would be even better."

Leada thanked Shrinker. She didn't know what Shrinker had told her. She thought he hadn't told her much, but she felt better. She was less tired.

She came to the Fuller furniture factory and asked to speak to Shaper. A handsome young man came out and said, "I'm Shaper." Leada said, "My name is Leada. I'm a customer. I have two Fuller chairs. I'm thinking of buying two more chairs and a table. I want to see how the chairs are made. Would you show me?" Shaper said, "I'll be glad to show you. Most customers don't care. They only want the furniture. They don't appreciate what goes into it. Everything we do is beautiful. Not only the furniture. But also the way it's made. Fuller designed it. Fuller furniture is the most beautiful furniture you can buy. It's the best made furniture you can buy. Do you realize that we use only wood. No nails. No screws. No metal of any kind. From beginning to end. The best wood there is."

Leada said, "Yes. It's beautiful. And the way the wood smells when you cut it. I always remember that smell." Shaper asked, "How come you remember the smell?" Leada said, "When I was little, my father did some wood work right in our house. I used to watch him. My mother didn't like it. But I liked nothing better than to watch him when he sawed the planks. Do you think I could try? Would you let me cut the next board?" Shaper said, "I don't know." Leada said, "Trust me. I've done it before. But your tools are so much better." Shaper said, "All right. But take your backpack off." Leada said, "What backpack? Oh, this one. I'm not allowed to take it off. I don't know why. But there's nothing in it. It's empty. It's so light I didn't even remember I had it on." Shaper said, "All right. I'll stand right next to you."

She picked up the board. She set the saw. She flipped the switch. One, two, three, and she had made all the cuts. Shaper said, "They're perfect. And so fast. Are you sure you've never worked in a furniture factory?" Leada said, "Honest. I never did. But I watched my father when I was small, and I did help him a little later on." Shaper said, "Any time you want a job, I'll hire you." Leada laughed happily, "Are you serious?" Shaper said, "Absolutely. It's very difficult to find people who know what to do with wood." Leada said, "You've made me very happy. But it's impossible. I'm doing other things." Shaper asked, "What things?" Leada said, "Just other things. But how about you? When did you start to work with wood?"

Shaper said, "I've worked with wood all my life. There was a time when I thought I would do something else, but I changed my mind." Leada asked, "What something else?" Shaper said, "Just something. It's not important." Leada said, "Thank you for showing me around. Thank you for letting me use the saw. It was a lot of fun."

Leada got back to the house around dinner time. When she saw Fuller, she asked, "May I take the backpack off now?" Fuller said, "Yes." Leada said, "The backpack didn't talk." Fuller said, "Perhaps it did, and you weren't paying attention." Leada said, "Will you explain it to me?" Fuller said, "We all carry an invisible backpack around with us all the time. It contains the should-wants in our life. You might think people would do what they want to do. You might think people would live the way they want to live. This is not so. Most people don't know what they want. They only know what they should want. After a while, they can't tell the difference.

"They don't eat the food they want. They eat the food they should want. They don't listen to the music they want to hear. They listen to the music they should want to hear. They don't live the way they want to live. They live the way they should want to live. Some of these should-wants are small. Some are large. The bigger they are, the more they weigh. They all go into the invisible backpack, and we carry them around on our back for the rest of our life. We don't notice them, because we're used to them. And the backpack gets heavier all the time.

"When we put on the talking backpack, all the should-wants go into it, and the talking backpack tells us about them." Leada said, "But it didn't talk." Fuller asked, "Didn't it get heavier and lighter at different times during the day?"

Leada said, "When I was on my way to Maya, the backpack was very heavy. I got very tired. When I left Maya, it was so heavy I had to sit down to rest. It was still heavy when I talked to Shrinker, but not as heavy as before. When I reached Shaper, it was light. It was so light I didn't even know I was wearing it." Fuller said, "So the backpack did talk." Leada said, "But it never said a word." Fuller said, "You didn't expect it to talk the way people talk, did you? It talked the way a backpack talks."

Next day, Leada asked Fuller, "Would you mind if I stopped studying to be a doctor?" Fuller asked, "Should I mind?" Leada said, "No. And would you mind if I went to work for Shaper in the factory?" Fuller asked, "Should I mind?" Leada said, "No." Fuller asked, "What made you decide so suddenly?" Leada smiled, and said, "When a talking backpack speaks, one must listen."

16. The Hollow-Brick Tower

Lark was a poet. When he wanted to write a new poem, he went for a walk. Sometimes, he didn't begin to think about his poem until he reached the river. Sometimes, he began as soon as he left his house.

One day, Lark was thinking while walking on the street. A man came hurrying toward him. The man wore a neat suit. With his left hand, he carried a big briefcase. With his right hand, he carried a cell-phone. He wasn't talking on the phone. He was just holding the phone in front of him. Neither Lark nor the man was watching where he was going. Lark was looking up into the air. The man was looking down at his phone. They bumped into each other real hard. The man dropped the phone. Lark said, "I'm sorry." The man didn't look at Lark. He got down on the ground, and moaned, "Oh my God, I dropped it. Did I break it? What's going to happen to me if it's broken?"

The open phone lay on the ground. It was a strange phone. It was green. There were no buttons to push. There was no place to listen. There was no place to talk. Maybe it wasn't a phone at all. It just had a square screen with an arrow on it. When the man saw that Lark was looking at the phone, he covered it with his hands. Lark tried to help the man get up. But the man said, "Just leave me alone." The man got up by himself, and walked away.

During the next few days, Lark looked more carefully at people carrying cell-phones on the street. One day, he saw a very fat man with a green phone. Lark thought it was the same kind of phone. This man too wore what looked like an expensive suit. He too carried a big briefcase. He too walked very fast. He too was just holding the phone in front of him. Now Lark was curious. He was curious about the strange phone. Maybe it wasn't a phone at all. He was curious about what the man was doing. He was curious about why the man was in such a hurry. Lark followed him.

The fat man went through many streets. He came to a dirt road and turned into it. A tall man with a big brief case came from the other direction. When Lark reached the dirt road, the fat man was ahead. The tall man was behind him. The fat man stopped. He bent down. He picked up something. Lark couldn't see what it was.

The tall man reached the fat man and gave him a big push. The fat man fell to the ground. The tall man took something away from the fat man. It was a brick. The tall man put the brick into his briefcase. He left the fat man lying on the ground.

When Lark got there, the fat man was brushing the dirt off his suit. Lark said, "Can I help you?" The fat man said, "I don't need any help. Go away." The fat man was still holding the green phone in his hand. Lark asked, "What kind of a phone is this?" The fat man quickly put the phone in his pocket. He said, "It's just a cell-phone. And it's none of your business."

On most evenings, Lark went to the Parlor. The Parlor is a place where people could buy things to eat and drink, and talk with their friends. When Lark had a new poem, he read it to the people at the Parlor. He usually read each poem on the day he wrote it. But there was one poem he had never read at the Parlor. It was a poem about dying. He thought people might not want to hear a poem about dying. He just kept this poem in the drawer of the table in his and Maya's bedroom.

One day Maya saw the poem in the drawer. She said, "Why didn't you ever read this poem at the Parlor? You wrote this poem when you were afraid of dying. Many people are afraid of dying. Your poem might help these people. I think you should read it."

That evening, Lark read the poem at the Parlor. After the reading, a handsome middle aged man came over to Lark and Maya's table. He asked, "May I join you?" Lark said, "Of course." The man said, "My name is Fuller. I'm a patient of Maya's." Lark asked, "Are you the Fuller who owns the furniture company?" Fuller said, "Yes. Maya's a very good doctor, but I'm sick, and she can't cure me. I've thought a lot about dying lately. You're a young man. I'm surprised you were able to write this poem. I want to give you a present. I have no use for this anymore."

Fuller took a green phone out of his pocket. He gave it to Lark, and continued, "This is a brickfinder. Many people try hard to get one.

Most of them never do. You'll have to find out for yourself what it's for. It could be good for you. It could be bad for you. Until this evening, I wasn't sure what I was going to do with it. I know it wouldn't be good for my son. I know it wouldn't be good for my daughter. I thought of throwing it away. But after hearing your poem, I think you might be able to use it wisely. Please be careful. If you have doubts, ask Maya. I'm not giving it to her because having it might upset her. But if you get in trouble, listen to what she says." Then Fuller got up and walked away. Maya asked, "What did he give you?" Lark said, "It looks like a green phone, but it isn't. Fuller called it a brickfinder. That's all I know. I'll find out."

Next morning, Lark went out. He held the brickfinder in front of him. An arrow appeared on the screen. He walked in the direction of the arrow. He came to a corner. The arrow pointed right. He turned in that direction. He made right turns and left turns when the arrow said to do so. Soon he didn't know where he was. Watching the arrow took all his attention. He came to a street with old buildings. There was a small pile of bricks on the sidewalk. The bricks must have been left there when a building was being repaired.

A very thin man stood next to the pile of bricks. He was the thinnest man Lark had ever seen. The man's face looked like a skull with a thin bit of skin stretched over it. When the man saw Lark, he came up to him and said, "Excuse me, sir. My name is Ferret. Please give me a job." Lark said, "This is ridiculous. I don't need anyone to work for me. And if I did, I wouldn't have the money to pay them." Ferret said, "Surely, you are joking, sir. A man in your position. Just let me work for you. I want to be your assistant."

Lark asked, "What do you do?" Ferret said, "I'm a shoemaker. I'm a very good shoemaker. But please, don't hold this against me, sir. I can do other things. I'm a very good manager. I'll help you run your business. I'll take care of your everyday problems. You won't have to worry about your money. You'll be free to do whatever you want to do."

Lark said, "I don't have any everyday problems. I don't worry about my money, because I don't have any. And I'm free to do whatever I want to do." Ferret said, "I can see you don't take me seriously. I feel bad when someone important like you makes fun of me. I'm only a shoemaker. I don't even have a job making shoes. But you shouldn't treat me badly just because I have nothing, and am nothing."

Lark cried out, "No. I'm sorry. You don't understand. I'm not making fun of you. I don't think less of you because you're a shoemaker. My very best friend is a shoemaker. I don't know who you think I am. I'm a poet.

I make a little money from my poems. My wife makes money as a doctor in the hospital. But we're not rich. I don't need help managing anything. There's nothing to manage."

Ferret said, "How can this be. You have a brickfinder." Lark said, "You know about the brickfinder? You know how it works? You know what it's for?" Ferret cried out, "You mean you have a brickfinder, and don't know what you have? You don't know what it does?" Lark asked, "Do you know?"

Ferret cried out, "This is the most amazing thing I've ever heard. Everyone in the world wants a brickfinder. Hardly anyone ever gets one. All my life I've hoped and prayed to have a brickfinder someday. You have one. And you don't know what you have, and it seems you don't care." Lark said, "Well, will you tell me?" Ferret said, "Yes. I'll tell you. And if I do, will you make me your assistant?" Lark said, "But I told you I have no money." Ferret said, "It doesn't matter. I'll work for you without pay. You'll pay me someday, whenever you want, whatever you want. I won't complain. I promise. Do we have a deal?" Lark said, "All right."

Ferret said, "I'll tell you in a moment. But let's not miss an opportunity. You followed the arrow here. Let's find the hollow brick. Go over there to this pile of bricks. When you hold the brickfinder above a hollow brick, you see a small circle instead of an arrow. When you come closer, the circle gets bigger. When you touch the brick, the circle fills the whole screen. Then you know you've found a hollow brick." Lark stepped up to the pile of bricks. There was no circle. The arrow pointed at the old building. Lark walked over to the building. He walked along the building. The arrow turned and pointed at the wall. Lark touched the wall. A circle appeared. Lark bent down. The circle grew larger. Lark touched a brick in the wall. It was about as far above the ground as Lark's knee. The circle filled the screen.

Ferret looked over Lark's shoulder, and said, "You've found one. It's too bad. It's part of the building. We won't take it." Lark asked, "You mean because we can't get it out of the wall?" Ferret said, "No. We could get it out of the wall if we wanted to. Some people do. But it's a bad thing to do. It's like stealing. I'd never do it myself. And as your assistant, I must convince you not to do it either." Lark said, "You won't find it hard to convince me."

Ferret said, "Let's go and find a quiet place where we can sit, and I'll tell you all about the brickfinder." They started to walk away. Just then a man in a suit came to the building. He was carrying a briefcase. He put the briefcase down, opened it, and took out something. Ferret said,

"You see, it's like I told you. He has a hammer and a chisel and a small drill. It'll take him a while, but he'll get the brick out. It's a shame. It's very sad. Some people will do anything. I don't know you well, but I don't think you're one of them. I wouldn't want to work for one of them. Now let's go."

They walked until they came to a small park. They sat down on a bench. Ferret began to speak. "A brickfinder leads you to hollow bricks. Actually, these bricks are not hollow at all. They're just called hollow. They look just like ordinary bricks. They weigh the same as ordinary bricks. But they are not ordinary bricks. When you find hollow bricks, you can build a hollow brick tower. That's not the kind of tower you build outside. It's a tower you build in a quiet safe place, right in your house where nothing will disturb it.

"The brick that's on the floor is called the base. It doesn't count. The smallest tower you can build is made of just two bricks, the base and one brick on top of it. That's called a one-story tower. You can build a tower of more bricks. A base and four bricks make a four-story tower. You can build maybe a seven or eight story tower. But when you add more stories, the tower becomes less steady. If any bricks fall, you must throw them out." Lark said, "All right. But what do you do with it? What's it for?"

Ferret said, "I'll tell you in a moment. I just have to explain one more thing first. If you use a base of only one brick, you can build it only so high. That's why people use a much bigger base. The bigger the base, the higher you can go. You could make a base of three or five, or even ten bricks. Or even twenty-five. The bigger the base, the more stories you can build. Do you see?" Lark said, "Yes. I see. And then what?"

Ferret said, "And then this. You take a hammer and tap the brick on top of the tower. You tap it gently, so you don't disturb the rest of the tower. The brick you tap breaks into tiny pieces. These pieces turn into money. They turn into a lot of money. A brick on top of a ten-story tower turns into ten times as much money as a brick on top of a one-story tower."

Lark said, "You could build a big tower. You could tap all the bricks, one after another. You could turn them all into money." Ferret said, "Why would anyone do this?" Lark said, "To get enough money to buy everything they want." Ferret laughed and said, "You still don't understand. Even if you tap only one brick on top of a one-story tower, you'll have enough money to buy anything you'll ever want." Lark asked, "Then why would you want to build a bigger tower?" Ferret answered, "You'd want to make sure that, no matter what you want, no matter what happens, you'll always have enough money. And, of course, there's another reason. People don't talk about this so much. But one always wants to have a bigger tower than other people. You can see that, can't you?" Lark didn't answer.

When Lark came home, he told Maya what he had found out. Maya listened. Then she said, "I'm worried, Lark." Lark asked, "What are you worried about?" Maya said, "I'm worried about you. I'm worried about us. I've seen people who have a lot of money. Often they don't live the way they should be living. They don't do what they should be doing. I don't think having a lot of money is a good thing."

Lark said, "It's not the money itself. Like Oaker says, it depends on who has it, and on what they do with it. Fuller said the same thing. He really wanted to give the brickfinder to you. But he knew it wouldn't be good for you. Please don't worry, Maya. If I do anything bad, tell me. Until then, just wait and see." Maya was not convinced, but she said, "All right."

Next morning, Ferret waited on the street in front of Lark's house. He was wearing a backpack. He said, "You'll have to get a big briefcase like all the others. In the meantime, I've brought a backpack, in case we find a hollow brick." Lark opened his brickfinder. They followed the arrow. They went a long distance. Finally, they turned into a dirt road. At the end of the road was the town dump. That's where people bring their garbage. The arrow pointed to the dump.

Ferret said, "We're very close now. I bet it's right inside." Lark said, "But we're not going in." Ferret asked, "Why not?" Lark said, "Because if we do, we'll get dirty." Ferret said, "I'm your assistant. If you don't want to go, I'll go in for you. Then you won't have to get dirty." Lark said, "No. If you're my assistant, I won't ask you to do anything I don't want to do myself." Ferret said, "Aren't you being picky? It's just a little dirt." Lark said, "I don't think I'm being picky. Yesterday, you said it would be wrong to take a brick from the wall of a building. It may not be wrong to take a brick from a garbage dump, but it's dirty. And I say, we won't take a brick from a place that'll make us dirty."

Ferret said, "I'm just the assistant. Maybe I agree. Maybe I don't. But I do what you tell me, because I promised. I keep my word." Lark said, "Thank you. We'll try again tomorrow."

Just then a man in a suit with a briefcase rushed past them. He climbed on the mountain of garbage and started to move things around. Lark and Ferret didn't know whether he found a brick. He was still moving things around when they left.

Next morning, Ferret was again waiting in front of Lark's house. The arrow of the brickfinder was pointing away from the river. Lark closed the cover of the brickfinder and said to Ferret, "All right. Let's go." Ferret asked, "Where are we going?" Lark said, "We're going down to the river." Ferret said, "But the arrow pointed in the other direction." Lark said, "That's true. But that's here in town. We don't know which way it'll point if we start by the river. Besides, I don't see too many men with suits and briefcases there." Ferret said, "Aha. You're very smart." Lark said, "I may be smart, but we're not going to the river because I'm smart. We're going there because it's a beautiful place to walk."

When they got to the river, Lark took out the brickfinder. The arrow pointed in the direction of the second bridge. As they were walking, Lark began to think about a new poem. They were almost past the bridge, when Ferret called out, "What are you doing? Where are you going? Aren't you watching? Here. Here." The arrow had turned.

Lark and Ferret climbed down to the river. There were a few loose bricks under the bridge. Lark put the brickfinder on one of them. A big circle appeared. Ferret called out, "That's one. We got one. We got a hollow brick." Lark picked up the brick, and put it into Ferret's backpack. He touched two more bricks. They were just ordinary bricks. The next one was a hollow brick. He put that one in Ferret's backpack too. After that, he touched all the bricks. He found one more hollow brick. He asked, "Can you carry all three?"

Ferret said, "Oh yes. They're not hard to carry in the backpack. This is amazing." Lark asked, "What's amazing?" Ferret said, "Some people spend all their time looking for hollow bricks. They think they're lucky when they find one. You're a beginner. And you've found three bricks the third time out. Just imagine how well you'll do once you have more practice." Lark said, "We'll see."

They walked back to Lark's house. Ferret asked, "Where do you want to start your tower?" Lark said, "I'll put it into the corner of our bedroom. It'll be safe there. No one will disturb it."

Ferret said, "These three bricks are a good beginning for a base." Lark said, "Actually, I'll use only one of them for the base." Ferret said, "This would be a big mistake. You can't enlarge the base after you've started. That's why smart people make a very big base. Then they can safely build a tower with many stories." Lark said, "But I'm not smart. I don't want a big base. And I don't want a tower with many stories. Just hand me the first brick, please." Ferret handed him the first brick. Lark put it on the floor in the corner. He said, "Now please hand me the second brick." Lark put the second brick on top of the first. He put the third brick on top of the second. Then he got up from the floor. He said,

"Come. We'll go into the other room. We'll sit where we can talk." Ferret was moaning, "A big mistake. This was a very big mistake." Lark smiled.

After they sat down, Lark said, "You've been a very good assistant. You told me how to build a hollow brick tower. You brought your backpack. You carried my hollow bricks home for me. Now I must pay you. Here. Take this brickfinder. It's yours." Ferret cried out, "You're joking. You can't do this. I can't accept this from you." Lark asked, "Why not?" Ferret said, "Because I haven't done anything. I don't deserve it."

Lark said, "You've seen all the people with briefcases and brickfinders. Do you think they've done anything? Do you think they deserve anything?" Ferret said, "They must have done something. They must deserve something, or they wouldn't have brickfinders." Lark said, "That's not how it is. We get what we get. Sometimes we work for it. Sometimes we're lucky. In the end, it's always because we're lucky. Don't worry about deserving. Luck comes. Luck goes. Don't be too proud when it comes. Don't cry too much when it goes. If you get something, take it, and be happy." Ferret took the brickfinder. He said, "Thank you very much," and left.

When Maya came home in the evening, she asked, "So what happened today? Did you find a brick?" Lark smiled, and said, "I didn't find just one brick. I found three. And I built us a hollow brick tower. It's just a two story tower, but we'll never have to be poor. We'll always have enough money to do anything we want to do."

Maya said, "I guess that's good. But what are you going to do tomorrow?" Lark said, "What do you mean, what am I going to do tomorrow? I'll go to the river, and I'll think about a poem." Maya said, "You will? But what about the brickfinder? What will you do with it?" Lark said, "I won't do anything with it. I gave it away."

Maya was surprised, and asked, "You gave it away? To whom?" Lark said, "I gave it to Ferret." Maya asked, "Why to him?" Lark said, "Ferret is an honest man. That's very rare. He'll make mistakes. In the end, I believe he'll use it well, and good will come of it."

Maya said, "When you got the brickfinder, I was worried. I was worried about what it would do to you. I was worried about what it would do to us. I always thought the more money people get, the more they want. I see now, it doesn't have to be that way." Lark said, "It's not over yet, Maya. We haven't used the money yet. We still don't know what the money will do to us. Either to you or to me. But I have great trust in us. We'll be all right." And he smiled.

17. The Leaf of Time

Ashly and Oaker lived in a log cabin. Their cabin was half way up a big mountain. There were trees in back of the cabin. There was a clearing in front of the cabin. A clearing has no trees, only grass. Sometimes, Ashly and Oaker walked to the edge of the clearing. They could see the town far below. Or they could look across and see the big mountains in the distance.

Ashly and Oaker did not look very old. Oaker was strong and handsome. Ashly liked him the way he was. But Oaker was going to be 80 years old on his next birthday. And Ashly knew that Oaker wanted to be young again. Ashly had once made Oaker a chain of acorns for his birthday. Oaker had liked the chain very much. Now Ashly wanted to make him a chain of acorns again. She thought that perhaps a chain of acorns would make Oaker feel young again. Acorns grow on oak trees. They look like nuts with little caps on. Squirrels like acorns. They pick up many acorns. They hide acorns to eat in the winter. But squirrels don't pick up all the acorns. When Ashly walked in the forest, she could always find some acorns the squirrels hadn't picked up.

One day, when Ashly was looking for acorns, she saw something under a tree. She bent down to look more closely. It was a squirrel. The squirrel did not move. It was hurt, but it was still alive. There was a dark spot on its fur and some blood around it. A hunter had shot the squirrel. Ashly did not like hunters. She did not want people to shoot living things for fun. She felt very sorry for the squirrel. When Ashly

touched the squirrel, the squirrel trembled all over. Ashly picked up
the squirrel. Squirrels don't let people pick them up, but this squirrel
was too weak to run away. It was breathing very hard. Ashly stroked
the squirrel gently and carried it home. She took a big scarf and made
a knot in it. Then she made a sling and put the squirrel in it. This way,
she could carry the squirrel in front of her while she walked. She told
Oaker that she had to go to the town.

At the hospital, Ashly told the nurse, "I have brought a squirrel here."
The nurse said, "This is a hospital for people, not for squirrels. You must
take the squirrel somewhere else." Ashly said, "I want to talk to a doctor.
I want to talk to Maya." When Maya came out and saw Ashly, she asked,
"What is the matter, Ashly? Are you all right? Is Oaker all right?" Ashly
said, "Yes, Maya. I am all right and Oaker is all right. But a hunter has
shot this squirrel." Maya said, "Come with me."

Maya looked at the squirrel and said, "You must hold the squirrel,
and keep it from moving. I will use tweezers to take out the bullet."
Ashly held the squirrel. It was breathing very hard. Maya put alcohol on
the tweezers to kill the germs. She pulled out the bullet. The squirrel was
shaking all over. Maya said, "Here is medicine. Put it into water. Use an
eyedropper to feed the squirrel. If you give it water and take care of it,
the squirrel may live."

Ashly thanked Maya and went back home. She took a box. She put
towels into the box and made a bed for the squirrel. She took very good
care of the squirrel.

When the squirrel was all better, Ashly thought to herself, "This
squirrel probably has a nest. That is the house where it lives. I must
take it back to the place where I found it, so it will be able to go home
again." Ashly picked up the squirrel. The squirrel was used to Ashly. It
let Ashly carry it. Ashly went through the forest. She went back to the
place where she had found the squirrel. She put the squirrel down on
the ground and said, "I hope you will be all right now." The squirrel answered, saying, "Thank you for saving my life."

Ashly was very surprised. Everyone knows that squirrels can't
speak. They can't make the sound of words with their mouth. But
the squirrel was not making sounds with its mouth. The squirrel was
speaking to Ashly in Ashly's mind. Ashly said, "I didn't know squirrels can speak." The squirrel said, "Of course we can speak. People
don't know this because we are not allowed to speak with humans. But
you were very good to me, and I want to do something for you before
I go home. Have you ever heard of a leaf of time?" Ashly said, "No."

The squirrel said, "You know that oak trees can grow very old." Ashly said, "Yes." The squirrel said, "When an oak tree gets to be 100 years old, it grows a leaf of time. Only one. Then it takes another hundred years before it grows another leaf of time. You can see that a leaf of time is very rare. Even in a big forest which has a lot of oak trees, it is very difficult to find an oak tree that is exactly 100 years old. And even if one finds it, it is very difficult to find the one leaf of time among all of the tree's many leaves. But I know where a leaf of time is, and I will help you get it."

Ashly asked, "But what is a leaf of time?" The squirrel answered, "You can spot a leaf of time by its color. It is a perfect gold. All leaves change color in the fall, but only a leaf of time is perfect gold." The squirrel then told Ashly all it knew about the leaf of time. Ashly asked many questions. After the squirrel had answered all of Ashly's questions, Ashly said, "I wanted to give Oaker a chain of acorns for his birthday. I wanted to make him feel young again. But I will give him the leaf of time instead." The squirrel said, "Don't you want to use the leaf of time for yourself?" Ashly said, "No. I have come to the forest to find a birthday present for Oaker. If I have found a leaf of time, then the leaf of time must be my present to him. But where is the leaf of time?"

The squirrel said, "I will lead you to the big oak tree that is just 100 years old. The leaf of time is high up. It is hidden among the leaves of the tree. You won't see it from the ground. But I will run up the trunk of the tree. I will jump across the branches until I reach the leaf of time. Then I will bite through its stem. The leaf will fall down and you will pick it up on the ground."

The squirrel led Ashly to a very big tree. It ran half way up the trunk of the tree. It stopped to make sure Ashly was there. Then it went higher and higher. It jumped from one branch to the next. Finally, it stopped on a branch high up on the tree. Ashly saw a flash of color. It appeared and disappeared. She looked very hard. She saw the color again. It was floating from side to side. It disappeared and appeared. Now she could see it was a leaf. She did not take her eyes off it. She followed it with her eyes. It came closer and closer. It reached the ground not far from where Ashly stood.

Ashly picked up the leaf. It was gold and perfectly shaped. It was the most beautiful leaf Ashly had ever seen.

The squirrel came down from the tree. It stood in front of Ashly and said, "Hold the leaf carefully, so it won't break. Write on it only with a real feather pen. Find a feather. Get a bottle of ink. When the time comes, dip the hard end of the feather into the ink and use the feather pen to write on the leaf of time." Ashly said, "Thank you for helping me find the leaf of time. I have been collecting acorns. I won't need them anymore. I will leave them behind the cabin. If you need acorns, you can find them there." The squirrel said, "I will come to get them, but I won't speak to you anymore. It is not allowed. I spoke to you this time only because you saved my life. Don't tell anyone that I spoke to you. But if you want to tell, go ahead and tell. No one will believe you anyhow. Everybody knows that squirrels can't talk. Ha, ha, ha. Goodbye." And the squirrel hopped away.

On the night before Oaker's birthday, Ashly put a tablecloth on the big wooden table. She put a large pottery plate in the middle of the table. She put the leaf of time on the pottery plate. She turned a second pottery plate upside down and put it over the leaf to hide it and protect it. She put a feather pen and a bottle of ink next to the plate.

Next morning she said, "Happy birthday, Oaker. I have a very special birthday present for you. Come with me into the other room." She asked Oaker to sit on a chair by the table. Then she asked, "Tell me, Oaker, do you want to be young again?" Oaker laughed and said, "Of course I want to be young again." Ashly said, "Look at me Oaker. I am not joking. I am serious. Do you know what age you would want to be?" Oaker saw that Ashly was serious and said, "I have thought sometimes that I want to be young again. But I have never thought about it carefully. I am not sure what age I would want to be." Ashly said, "You must think about it very carefully now. Here is a feather pen and ink." She lifted the top plate off, and said pointing, "And this is a leaf of time. It is the birthday present I am giving you."

Oaker asked, "What is a leaf of time?" Ashly answered, "A leaf of time is very special. If you have a leaf of time, you don't have to just think about being younger. You can pick any age you want. If you dip the feather pen into the ink and write an age on the leaf of time, you will be that age. If you want to be 20 years old again, all you have to do is write the number 20 on the leaf of time, and you will be 20 years old." Oaker asked, "For how long? Just for a short time? Just to see what it feels like?" Ashly answered, "No. A leaf of time isn't just a trick. It isn't just a way of helping you imagine what it was like to be 20. If you write 20 on a leaf of time, you will really be 20 years old again." Oaker asked, "Will I get older again?" Ashly said, "Yes, you will start to live the rest of your life from the age you picked." Oaker asked, "Will I remember everything I know?" Ashly answered, "Yes, you will remember. But perhaps this will not help you much. You will be the age you picked. You will have the mind of a person of that age. And you will not think about what has happened to you the way you think about it today. You will think about it the way you would have thought about it when you were the age you picked. And now I will be quiet. Please sit here, Oaker, and think about it. Think about it very carefully because it is very important. Pick an age. Don't say anything. Just write the age you picked on the leaf of time."

Oaker leaned back in his chair. He closed his eyes and started to think about his life.

When Oaker was 5 years old, it was a good time. He had a tree house. When Oaker was 8 years old, it was a good time. He read many books. He learned to ice skate. When Oaker was 10 years old, it was a good time. He explored the forest with his friends. But Oaker didn't want to remain 5 years old, or 8 years old, or 10 years old. He wanted to grow up.

When Oaker was 20 years old, it was a good time. He had many girl friends. He had a lot of fun. He thought that he had everything he wanted. But he was often very sad.

When Oaker was 30 years old, it was a good time. He found Ashly. He liked her better than any of his other girl friends. They got married and had two children, a boy and a girl. But they were very poor and worried a lot.

When Oaker was 40 years old, it was a good time. Oaker built houses for people. He drew plans. He hired people to help him, carpenters, plumbers, electricians. But he wanted to build big buildings.

When Oaker was 50 years old, it was a good time. He was famous. People came to him from far away. He built a city hall and a library and a school and a church and a temple. But he was often away and couldn't be with Ashly.

When Oaker was 60 years old, it was a good time. Every weekend, Ashly and Oaker went on a hike. They found a clearing they liked, half way up a mountain. They made picnics. But they couldn't spend much time there.

When Oaker was 70 years old, it was a good time. Ashly and he wanted to move to their favorite clearing, half way up the mountain. They built a cabin all by themselves. They cut down trees. They put the logs together. They made tables and chairs and beds. But Oaker began to be afraid of getting old.

Now Oaker and Ashly lived in their cabin. They liked living there. The leaf of time was on the table in front of him. And Oaker had to pick an age. He wanted to be younger, but he wasn't sure which age to pick. Then he saw Ashly's face across from him. He picked up the feather pen, dipped it into the ink, and wrote the number 80 on the leaf of time. The number began to glow. It became a number of fire. The fire spread. The whole leaf burned and only a little heap of ashes was left.

Ashly said, "Why didn't you pick an age?" Oaker said, "I did." Ashly said, "I wanted to give you a very special present." Oaker said, "You did." Ashly said, "You didn't use my present." Oaker said, "I did." Ashly said, "How did you use my present?" Oaker said, "Before you gave me the leaf of time, I was sure I wanted to be young again. But now I know that I don't want to go back to where I have been. I don't want to do what I have already done. Thank you, Ashly for the wonderful present you gave me. Thank you, Ashly for helping me understand that every age is good." Ashly was happy. She cried and smiled at the same time.

Oaker put his arm around Ashly. They went out of the cabin to the edge of the clearing. They looked down and saw the town far below. They looked across and saw the mountains in the distance. The sun was rising over the mountains. It was very beautiful.

18. The Prism for Rings

Maya was a doctor at the hospital. Fuller was the owner of the Fuller furniture company. He was one of Maya's patients. If you just looked at him, you couldn't tell there was anything wrong with him. But he was sick. The last time he had seen Maya, she had taken blood. Now he was back to find out what the tests showed. Maya asked, "How are you doing?" Fuller said, "I'm all right, but I get tired." Maya came around from behind her desk, and sat next to Fuller. She said, "I'm sorry. It's going to get worse. The tests show you are sick. They are worse than last time."

Fuller asked, "Am I going to die?" Maya said, "We're all going to die." Fuller said, "You know what I mean. Am I going to die soon? Very soon?" Maya said, "I'm only a doctor. I'm not God. My opinion could be wrong. Besides, people often ask, but they don't want to know." Fuller said, "I want to know." Maya said, "You'll get worse. You'll become weaker. It'll become more difficult to move your arms and legs. In the end, you may not be able to move them at all." Fuller asked, "How long?" Maya said, "I told you, I don't know." Fuller asked, "A year? A month? A week?" Maya said, "Maybe three months. Maybe a little more. Maybe a little less. I'm sorry." Fuller said, "Thank you, Maya," and left.

That evening, there was a knock on the door of Lark and Maya's house. Fuller said to Lark, "I'm sicker than I thought. Maya can't help me. There's no medicine for me. I could go on this way, but it'll only get worse. I don't want to do this. I've thought about it all day. There's nothing else to do. I must turn to magic. Will you do me a favor?" Lark said, "I'll do anything I can."

Fuller said, "Oaker and Ashly are friends. I need something they may have. I can't go up myself. If I just walk from here to the next street, I'm out of breath. Going up the mountain is impossible. Please go up for me. Tell them I'm sick. Ask them whether they have a prism for rings. If they do, please bring it to me. You can bring it to my house tomorrow evening." Lark asked, "What's a prism for rings?" Fuller said, "I'll tell you what it is, but not now. Let's find out whether Oaker and Ashly have one. And one more thing. Tell them I'm having a dinner party at my house, Sunday afternoon at five o'clock. I hope they'll come. You and Maya are invited too."

Next morning, Lark hiked up to Oaker and Ashly's cabin. Oaker said, "We have a prism for rings. Tell Fuller, we'll come to his dinner party on Sunday." Ashly left the room. She brought back a shiny small pyramid on a thin chain. She said, "Don't wear it yourself. Don't even try it on. It's for Fuller only. I'll wrap it in this handkerchief. This way, you'll be able to carry it safely in your pocket." Lark asked, "What is it? What's it for?" Oaker said, "Fuller will tell you. If he doesn't, I will. In the meantime, just take it to him. All right?" Lark said, "All right. Have you known Fuller long?"

Oaker said, "Yes. We've been friends for many years. Like Shrinker, he was a member of the oval circle." Lark asked, "Isn't that where you learned to do magic?" Oaker laughed, "One doesn't do magic. Magic is part of the world. Our teacher only taught us to see this more clearly. But I think you know this already."

When Lark came home, Maya asked, "Did Oaker have the thing Fuller wanted?" Lark said, "Yes. Here it is." He took the handkerchief out of his pocket. He opened it. He showed Maya the prism and the chain. She said, "I wonder why he wants it. I wonder what it does." Lark said, "I'm going to bring it to him now. Come along with me." Maya said, "All right. I'll come. He's a very sick man. I want to know what he's going to do with it."

Lark and Maya went to Fuller's house. Beava opened the door. Beava was a very big woman. Very big people sometimes move slowly, but Beava moved fast. She was Fuller's housekeeper. She saw to it that the house was always clean, and that everything that needed to be done was taken care of. Fuller also had a chef, Gobbler, who did all the cooking. Gobbler was a very good chef. Everything he made was delicious.

Beava led Lark and Maya into the dining room. It was a large room, with a big, heavy oak table. The top of the table was as thick as a thick book. Lark wondered how many men it had taken to carry the table into the house. One side of the dining room had windows that looked out into a garden. It was at the edge of steep rocks. One could see nothing but the garden and the rocks beyond. On the far side of the dining room was an old fashioned clock. It had a pendulum that went back and forth. The clock was almost as high as the ceiling. It was the kind of clock that rings at the beginning of each hour.

Fuller was sitting at the end of the table, opposite the clock. He was just finishing his dinner. When Lark and Maya came in, he got up, and said, "Please sit down. Would you like some tea or coffee and dessert?" They said they didn't want anything, but they sat down. Fuller asked, "Did Oaker have a prism?" Lark took out the handkerchief. He gave Fuller the chain with the prism. Fuller looked at it, and said, "Very good, Lark. Thank you." Lark asked, "What are you going to do with it?" Fuller said, "Put it on, and wear it, of course. I'll wait two more minutes. I'll put it on at exactly eight o'clock." Maya asked, "But what is it for? What will it do?"

Just then the clock sounded. Fuller said, "Here we are. It's eight o'clock." He put the chain with the prism around his neck. He smiled happily, and said, "And do you know what I'm going to do now?" Maya and Lark didn't know. Fuller said, "I'm going for a long walk. Excuse me while I get a sweater."

When he left the room, Maya said, "We can't let him go. He's very sick. He's very weak. He might fall on the way." Lark said, "He's a grown man. We can't stop him if he wants to go." Maya said, "Then let's go with him and keep an eye on him."

Fuller came back. Lark said, "We're going home. Come, walk with us as far as our house." Fuller said, "I'll be glad to. Let's go." Fuller led the way. He took big steps. He walked fast. Lark was used to walking. But it was hard for him to keep up with Fuller. Maya had to skip and hop along. She was surprised. When they came to Lark and Maya's house, Fuller said goodbye and went on. Lark and Maya looked after him. Maya said, "He looks strong. He doesn't look tired. I don't understand it. But I don't think he needs us."

Fuller walked on. After a while, he passed the Parlor. That's a place where people eat, drink, and talk with friends. He went in. He got tea and a plate of cookies. He looked for a place to sit. He saw a young woman alone at a table. He liked her looks. He went over to her. He didn't know her, but he said, "You look very familiar. May I sit with you?" She smiled at him, and said, "I'll be happy if you sit with me. But I believe you're just pretending." Fuller asked, "What makes you think so?"

She said, "I'm a witch. I can read minds." Fuller said, "Really? That's interesting. Show me." She put her hands to her forehead. Fuller thought she looked beautiful. She said, "I see a glass. There's water in it. The glass is full. Your name must be Fuller."

Fuller said, "Tell me more." She put her hands to her forehead again. She said, "I see a young woman. She's your daughter. Her name is Leada." Fuller said, "That's very good. But I don't believe you're a witch." She asked, "Why not?" Fuller said, "I've known real witches. I can tell the difference between a real witch and a pretend witch." She said, "You can? What's the difference?" Fuller said, "There are ugly witches and there are pretty witches. But even a pretty witch wouldn't be as beautiful as you."

She said, "Maybe I'm not a full witch yet. Maybe I'm in training. Maybe I'm only a half witch." Fuller said, "I don't believe you're a full witch. And I don't believe you're a half witch. I believe you work in the office of my furniture company." She said, "So you recognized me?" Fuller said, "No. I'm sorry. I didn't recognize you. But it's obvious." She asked, "It is?" Fuller said, "Of course. You knew my name. You knew my daughter's name. You must have seen me when I didn't know it. That must have been in the office. What's your name?" She said, "My name is Lily. You're right. You always walked through the typing area where I worked. I saw you. But you never paid attention to me. You never even knew I was there."

Fuller said, "So you're a typist?" Lily said, "Actually, I'm not a typist anymore. After Leada took over your job, she called me in one day. She talked to me a long time. Then she made me manager of the department." Fuller asked, "How's she doing?" Lily said, "All right. But there's always good and bad." Fuller asked, "What's the good." Lily said, "When you were in charge, you never talked to any of the people. You only talked to the managers. Leada knows all the people who work in the company. She knows their names. She talks to them. They all like her. That's the good." Fuller asked, "And the bad?" Lily said, "She admires you a lot. She tries hard to do everything the way you did it." Fuller asked, "And that's bad?" Lily said, "Yes. Because the one thing she doesn't realize is that you changed things all the time. So the more she tries to keep things the same, the more different they become." Fuller looked at Lily, and said, "Leada was very smart to make you a manager. I think you'll help her a lot." Lily looked into his eyes, and said, "I really try to help."

Fuller felt a warm feeling for Lily. He reached across the table. He took her hand in his. He said, "I haven't felt this good in a very long time, Lily. There's no place I'd rather be right now than here with you." Lily said, "I'd rather be somewhere else." Fuller was still holding her hand. Lily reached across the table, and took his other hand. Now they were holding both hands across the table. She said, "I've baked much better cookies than these. I'd rather be with you in the place where I live." Fuller got up, and said, "All right. Let's go." Lily put her arm through his, and they walked out.

Lily made tea. She put cookies on the table. She said, "I can't believe it. I can't believe you're actually here in my place." Fuller asked, "What's so surprising about it?" Lily said, "It's like a dream come true. Don't you realize, this is all the girls in the office ever talked about. After your wife died, they all said they were going to talk to you. But then Leada took over your job, and you didn't come to the office anymore. They would all be jealous if they knew I was here with you." Fuller asked, "But why?" Lily said, "For a smart, important man, you don't know very much. They all wanted to be your girlfriend."

Fuller asked, "And how about you?" Lily said, "Girls are that way. When the boss of a company is smart and handsome, they all want to be his girlfriend." Fuller asked, "And how about you?" Lily said, "Gossip, gossip, gossip. That's what goes on in the office all day long. Everybody sticks their nose into everybody else's business. The answer is, yes." Fuller asked, "Yes, what?" Lily said, "Yes. I also wanted to be your girlfriend. I especially. More than the others. I thought of it all the time."

Fuller said, "I'm old enough to be your father." Lily said, "You don't look old to me. But that's not the point. Don't you want me to be your girlfriend?"

Fuller said, "I would like it very much. But it's impossible." Lily asked, "Why?" Fuller said, "I won't be able to stay with you. I'm going away on a long trip. Then you won't see me anymore, and you'll feel bad."

Lily said, "I'm not asking for promises. If it doesn't last, it doesn't last. But right now, I want to be your girlfriend." Fuller said, "I'll be going away very soon. Then you'll be mad at me. I don't want you to be mad at me. I don't want to hurt you." Lily said, "I'll take my chances. I'd rather do that than never be your girlfriend at all." Fuller said, "Will you remember later that I warned you?" Lily said, "I'll feel very sad if you go away. But I won't be mad at you. I promise, I'll remember." Fuller gave Lily a big hug and said, "I'm very happy." Lily gave Fuller a big hug, and said, "I'm more happy than you."

Next morning was Friday. Lily was making breakfast when Fuller woke up. She said, "I got up early. Stari lives nearby. I went to her house. I asked her to tell them I won't be in the office today. I want to be with you, if you want." Fuller said, "Of course, I want. Is there anything special you want to do today?" Lily said, "No. How about you?" Fuller said, "I would like to make a picture of you. I could work on the picture during the day. We could eat dinner at my house. Gobbler will make us a very good dinner. And we could go walking by the river in the evening." Lily said, "That sounds wonderful."

Two wide steps led to the front of Fuller's house. First one came into a foyer. This was a large room with a stone floor. A hall on the left led to Fuller's bedroom and studio. A hall on the right led to the dining room, the kitchen, and to rooms beyond where Beava and Gobbler lived. The living room was straight ahead. Big windows looked out at trees. One could see mountains in the distance. One of the walls was made of stone. It had a large fireplace. There were pictures everywhere, pictures of people, pictures of mountains, pictures of streets of the town.

Lily asked, "Who made all these pictures?" Fuller said, "I made them." Lily asked, "When did you make them?" Fuller said, "Years ago. I haven't made any pictures for a long time. But now I want to make a picture of you." Fuller's studio was right next to his bedroom. Fuller told Lily to look around the house while he got ready. When she came back, he said, "Please sit still while I draw a picture of you on the canvass. Then you can move around. If you want, you can watch me put on the paint. I'll ask you to sit still a few more times. I hope you won't be bored." Lily said, "I won't be bored. I'll just watch you."

Fuller worked for two hours. They had a delicious lunch in the dining room. He continued after lunch. Then he said, "Now I'll let the paint dry. If it's OK with you, I'll finish the picture on Sunday. We can do anything you want tonight and tomorrow." Lily said, "Could we go for a walk by the river like you said?" Fuller said, "Sure. And how about tomorrow?" Lily said, "I work in an office all week. On the weekend, I like to be outside. Could we go up a mountain?"

Fuller gave Lily a big hug. He laughed, and said, "That's perfect. The one thing I want to do more than anything else is go up a mountain." Lily said, "We'll take backpacks and make a picnic. And we won't stay out too late tonight, because we'll have to get up early in the morning."

Saturday morning, Fuller and Lily got up early. Lily picked a small mountain. She wanted to reach the top by midday, so they could have the picnic there. They hiked through the forest. They stopped to rest. They drank water. They climbed higher and higher. They came out of the forest to a rocky meadow. They could see a long way. They could see the forest below. They could see the mountains in the distance. The sun was shining, but it wasn't hot. Fuller said, "Thank you for bringing me here. When I climb a mountain, when I breathe the fresh air, when I look into the distance, I feel I'm going to live forever." They had the picnic on top of the mountain. They lay down on blankets and looked up at the sky. The small white clouds looked very close.

On Sunday, Fuller worked on the picture again. By the afternoon, it was finished. Lily wanted to go back to her place to get a different dress for the dinner party. Fuller went with her. They walked holding hands. They were dressed and ready by five o'clock.

Oaker and Ashly came first. Then Lark and Maya came. Then Fuller's daughter Leada and her husband came. Leada was surprised when she saw Lily with her father. But she was pleased. She said to her father, "You are very lucky." Fuller said, "I know." Fuller's son, Seeker and his girlfriend came last. Leada said her brother was always late. They sat down to dinner before six o'clock.

Beava brought in the first course, tiny shrimp in Russian dressing on lettuce. There was sparkling water and wine. Gobbler didn't use any foods that were prepared anywhere else. He cooked and baked everything himself, including the bread and the crispy rolls.

Fuller told the story of the house. Oaker had built it. It had taken more than a year to build, and they hadn't argued once. Oaker told them that in the beginning Fuller had designed furniture, tables, chairs, benches, chests for himself. People had liked that furniture so much that Fuller had started his furniture company. Beava brought in soup. It was made of summer squash and carrots, and just a little ginger, with no milk or cream. It was soft and smooth and silky. Everyone liked it.

Seeker turned to his father and said, "You're wearing a chain with a shiny pyramid. What is it?" Just then Beava brought in the next course, cold poached salmon with cucumbers all around. Everyone admired it.

Beava walked around the table. She put a piece of salmon on every plate, with cucumber salad and green mayonnaise.

Ashly asked Lily when Fuller and she had met. Lily said, "Only three days ago. I can't believe it. It seems like a lifetime to me."

Beava brought in the next course. There were three meats, duck with orange sauce and wild rice, sweet glazed ham with snap peas, and breaded veal cutlets with lemon and roasted potatoes. Everyone took some of each.

Ashly asked Lily, "How often do you go to the Parlor?" Lily said, "That's the strange thing. I don't go often at all, perhaps once every two or three weeks. I didn't plan to go on Thursday. I was tired when I came home from work, and just lay down. I must have fallen asleep. I don't think I slept more than ten minutes. But I had a dream. I dreamt I was at the Parlor. People told me I had won a prize. That was strange. I don't do anything for which I could get a prize. But I was no longer tired. Suddenly I felt I should go to the Parlor. I don't know why. But I know it's the best thing I ever did."

Beava brought coffee and tea, and dessert. There were three desserts. Gobbler had just baked them. There was a flourless almond cake with a chocolate glaze. There was a Napoleon with rich cream between crispy layers of pastry. And there was an apple strudel with delicious green apples inside, and a flaky crust around. Everyone took some of each dessert. Fuller asked, "Has everyone had enough?" They all said, yes.

Then Fuller waved to Beava. She came in with a big lemon cake. Fuller asked Seeker, "Do you like lemon cake?" Seeker said, "You know it's my favorite." Fuller asked, "Do you want a piece?" Seeker answered, "I've just had a wonderful meal. I couldn't eat another thing."

Then Fuller waved to Beava, and she brought in a big chocolate cake. He turned to Leada and asked, "Do you like chocolate cake?" Leada said, "I don't know what you are doing, dad. You know it's my favorite dessert." Fuller asked, "Well, do you want any?" Leada said, "That's not nice of you, dad. You know I couldn't eat a thing now. If I did, I'd probably never like chocolate cake again."

Fuller waved to Beava. She took the desserts away. Then Fuller said, "You've seen that I'm wearing this chain with the shiny pyramid. Lark asked about it. Seeker asked about it. Now I'll tell you about it. But first, I must tell you something else. I'm very sick. Maya is my doctor. She did many tests. They were all bad. The pyramid I'm wearing is a prism for rings. Every day of a person's life is made up of rings. There are two kinds of rings. There are crystal rings. These are the rings of health and life. And there are black rings. These are the rings of sickness and death. If we have mostly crystal rings, we are healthy. If we have mostly black rings, we are sick. An ordinary prism separates red light from blue light. A prism for rings separates crystal rings from black rings.

The particular prism I'm wearing is a three day prism. It has collected all the crystal rings from the remainder of my life, and has put them into just three days. It has collected all the black rings from these three days, and put them into the remainder of my life. That's why I've been so healthy these past three days. It's a choice I made. I could have chosen a seven day prism, or a five day prism. I chose a three day prism, because I wanted to be completely healthy once more. These three days have been wonderful three days. And you must know…" Just then, the clock sounded. It was eight o'clock. Fuller leaned back in his chair. His mouth was open. Lily cried out, "What must we know, Fuller? Fuller? What's the matter, Fuller?" Maya got up. She checked Fuller's pulse. She listened to his chest. Then she said, "Fuller is dead."

Lily and Leada began to cry. Oaker got up. He closed Fuller's eyes. He picked him up, and carried him to the sofa. He went into the other room. He came back with a blanket and covered Fuller. Then he went back to the table.

Leada asked Maya, "How sick was he?" Maya said, "He was very sick." Leada asked, "How long would he have lived without the prism?" Maya said, "Maybe three months." Leada asked, "Then why did he do it?" Oaker said, "He told you why he did it." Leada asked, "He did? When did he tell us?"

Oaker said, "This entire meal was his way of telling you. His life was like this feast. He enjoyed his life, and especially the last three days, the way you enjoyed this feast and especially the three desserts. But you didn't want to go on and eat more and more when you no longer could. That would have made you hate the cake you like. And he didn't want to go on, and become weaker and sicker. That would have made him hate the life he liked."

Lily said, "He told me he would have to go on a trip. I promised I would remember that he told me. I will." Seeker said, "But why did he choose such a short time? Only three days." Oaker said, "It doesn't matter whether it's three days, or three months, or three years, or thirty years. When it's over, it's all the same. The only thing that matters is how you filled the time. Fuller was a very lucky man. He had three days in which he got everything. He got someone he liked who liked him. He made a picture. And he climbed a mountain."

19. The Nervous Rubber Heart

T hree days after Fuller died, a stranger came to Lark's house. He wore a suit and carried a briefcase. He said, "My name is Fixer. I have been Fuller's lawyer for many years. How well did you know Fuller?" Lark said, "My wife, Maya, was his doctor. But she couldn't help him. He came to the Parlor where I read my poems. He was very good to me. He gave me a present. And he invited Maya and me to his dinner party last Sunday. We were there when he died. Why do you ask?"

Fixer didn't answer. Instead, he asked, "Did Fuller say anything to you about what he wanted to happen after he died?" Lark said, "No." Fixer said, "Very strange. Last Thursday, Fuller came to my office. He told me to find you after he died, and to give you this letter. He also signed many papers. He wanted to make sure it would all be legal. Did you know that he knew more law than many lawyers?" Lark said, "No. I knew that he founded the furniture company. I knew that he designed the furniture. I knew that he made beautiful pictures. I knew that he was a wise man."

Fixer shook his head. "He did strange things. When I tried to warn him, he smiled and said, 'Don't worry. Please just do what I ask you to do. It'll be all right.' And it always worked out. But I think this time he went too far." Lark asked, "What did he do?" Fixer said, "Here. Read this." And he handed Lark the letter.

The letter said, "Dear Lark, I am writing this on Thursday morning. I believe you are now on your way to Oaker and Ashly's cabin. I believe they have the prism for rings. They will know that I'm asking them for a three-day prism because I'm inviting them to a dinner party on Sunday, which is three days from today. They will understand what this means. By the time you read this, you will understand it too. Now, I'm asking you for a favor, and am sending you a present.

"You know my two children. Leada is the head of the furniture company. Seeker is a philosopher. You also know my housekeeper, Beava, and my chef, Gobbler. I own the furniture company, the house, and a hollow brick tower in the corner of my studio. I'm not writing down who should get what. I want you to decide. My lawyer, Fixer is an honest man. I've told him to do anything you ask him to do. He thinks this is terrible. He warns me that I don't know you well. But I know you better than one might think. I know you are Maya's husband. I know some of your poems. And I know what you did with the brickfinder. Maya told me. You are still young, but you were wiser than I. Go to my studio. You'll find a hollow brick tower there. You'll know what to do. Talk to everyone. Fixer will ask them to be at the house on Sunday, one week after I die. Talk to them then.

"Fixer has a little box for you. Inside is a Nervous Rubber Heart. Pin it to your shirt. Find out yourself what it's for. When you're sure you don't need it anymore, give it to someone who does. It's wonderful to be young. Goodbye, my young friend, goodbye."

Fixer had watched silently while Lark was reading. Now he gave him a little box. There was a pin inside. It was a small red rubber heart. Lark pinned it to his shirt. Then he asked Fixer, "Have you been to the house?" Fixer said, "I've been there. I've told Beava to leave everything just the way it is until next Sunday. I also told her to let you into the house. You're free to do anything you want there. I don't understand it, but that's what Fuller wanted. I hope he was right." Lark smiled and said, "I hope so too. I'll be at your office later today or tomorrow morning. Thank you." Fixer shook his head, and left.

Lark went to see Shrinker, and said, "I believe you know that Fuller is dead." Shrinker said, "Yes. I'm very sad." Lark showed Shrinker the red heart. He asked, "Do you know what this is?" Shrinker said, "Yes. It's a nervous rubber heart." Lark asked, "Do you know what it's for?" Shrinker said, "Yes." Lark asked, "Could you tell me what it's for?" Shrinker asked, "Where did you get it?" Lark said, "Fuller left it for me." Shrinker said, "I could tell you what it's for, but I won't. You must discover this yourself.

"In the old days, the nervous rubber heart was the final test. We had to discover what it's for. When we thought we knew, we had to tell our teacher. We had to be sure we knew the answer, because there was no second chance. If our answer was right, we were allowed to join the oval circle. When you think you've discovered what the nervous rubber heart is for, come back. I'll tell you whether you're right.

"Of course, our teacher is dead now, and Fuller is dead, and there is no oval circle anymore. But you'll know whether you could have become a member in those days. How old are you, Lark?" Lark said, "I'll be thirty on my next birthday." Shrinker said, "Who knows, maybe there'll be another oval circle someday in your lifetime." Lark asked, "What was the point of the oval circle?" Shrinker said, "The members of the oval circle didn't just use magic that was known. They discovered and created new magic."

Lark went back home. He took a hammer and a backpack. He went to Fuller's house. Beava came to the door. Her eyes were red. She had been crying. "Isn't it terrible," she said, "It was so sudden. We knew that he was sick. But he was so strong, so full of life. I can't believe he isn't here anymore. Every moment, I expect to hear him asking me for coffee, or to have his suit fixed. He always said please and thank you. He never made us feel that we just worked in his house. He always treated Gobbler and me like family. What will become of us now? Please sit down, Lark. Gobbler will fix you some lunch." Lark said, "Thank you, Beava. I'll have some tea and something. But I don't want to sit in the dining room. If it's all right with you, I'd like to come to the kitchen." Beava said, "Of course, it's all right. Fixer said Fuller wanted us to treat you like we would have treated Fuller himself."

They went into the kitchen. Gobbler got up. Beava introduced them. Lark said, "The feast you made last Sunday was the best meal I've ever had." Gobbler smiled bitterly, and said, "I tried very hard and then it had this terrible end." Lark said, "But you did well." Gobbler said, "How can you say I did well when Fuller died right at the end of the meal I made." Lark said, "Your meal was exactly what Fuller wanted. It made him very happy. Fuller knew that he was going to die when the clock struck eight. He planned it that way. Didn't anyone tell you?" Gobbler asked, "He knew? Really?" Lark said, "Yes."

Gobbler said, "I've been Fuller's chef for over twenty years. Beava and I started to work for him when the house was built. I've felt terrible that the meal I made brought him bad luck." Lark said, "The meal you made was good luck. He wanted to give his guests a meal they would remember. You helped him do it. You helped him die exactly the way he wanted to die. Few people have this privilege." Gobbler began to cry. Over and over he sobbed, "Thank you, Lark. Thank you."

Beava said, "Why don't you fix something for Lark." Lark had tea and a piece of chocolate cake. As Gobbler served him, he asked, "What's going to happen to us? Are we going to have to leave?" Lark asked, "Do you want to leave?" Gobbler said, "This has been my home for over twenty years. This has been my job for over twenty years. I think I've done a good job. I think Beava has done a good job. But that won't make a difference. The children don't need the house. They'll probably sell it. Then we'll have to leave. This makes me sad." Beava said, "Me too."

Lark thanked Beava and Gobbler. He walked to the other end of the house. He found Fuller's bedroom and studio. There was an easel in the studio. There was a picture of Lily on the easel. Lily's face had a soft glow. It was slightly pink. Her dress was also pink. The background was in deep colors, green, blue, purple. The colors of the figure and dress were bright and cheerful. The colors of the background were sad. They weren't really dark, but they made you think of the dark. Lark thought it was a beautiful picture.

In one corner of the room, Lark saw the hollow brick tower. Lark was surprised. It was only a one-story tower. Fuller had had the brick-finder for a long time, but he hadn't used it. Lark took the hammer out of the backpack and gently tapped the top brick. The brick crumbled into tiny pieces. Each little piece turned into money. There was a mountain of money. Lark had never seen so much money. It was a good thing that his backpack was large. He opened it and put the money into the backpack. He had to push and squeeze to get the zipper closed, but he got it all in. He tapped the second brick. The brick crumbled. It turned into fine dust. It didn't turn into money. That's how a hollow brick tower works. Only the bricks above the base turn into money.

Lark said goodbye to Beava. He went directly to Fixer's office. Fixer's desk was on one side of the office. A big table was on the other side. Lark took off his backpack. He opened it. He started to stack the money on the table.

Fixer came over from behind his desk, and cried out, "My God, what are you doing? Where did you get all this money?" Lark said, "This is Fuller's money. I've brought it here so you can put it into a bank for him."

Fixer said, "But I can't just take it like that. How much is there?" Lark said, "I don't know." Fixer was upset. "This is a large amount of money. It must be counted. It must be counted very carefully." Lark said, "Go ahead. Count it." Fixer said, "No. I can't do the counting. What if I took some of it? It must be counted by others. By two people. I'll call two of my assistants."

He went to the door, and two young people came in. Fixer told them that each of them had to count the money. He said to Lark, "You must stay here until it's all counted. You must watch while they count it. Both of us must watch. Then I'll give you a receipt." Lark said, "I don't need a receipt." Fixer said, "Yes, you need a receipt. What if I said later you never gave me the money? What would you do then?" Lark said, "But you wouldn't say that. You're an honest man." Fixer said, "There's no such thing as an honest man. A man can be honest and honest and honest. He can be honest all his life. Then one day, he's suddenly not honest anymore. Fuller never understood this. It seems you don't understand it either. You're just as bad as Fuller." Lark was pleased. He liked to be compared to Fuller.

The two assistants were busy counting at the table. Fixer watched them while he continued to talk with Lark. He said, "Birds of a feather flock together. I thought he was making a terrible mistake when he left everything up to you. Maybe he knew what he was doing. He belonged to a group of magicians. Do you belong to that group too?" Lark said, "That's right."

Suddenly there was a loud buzzing in the room. At first, Lark didn't know where the buzzing was coming from. Neither Fixer nor his assistants paid attention to it. Then Lark realized that the buzzing was coming from the heart he wore on his chest. He was amazed that such a little heart was making so much noise. He asked Fixer, "Do you hear a buzzing sound?" Fixer stopped, listened, and said, "No. I don't hear anything. Why do you ask?" Lark said, "I thought I heard something."

Lark wondered why the nervous heart had started to buzz suddenly. He had told Fixer that he was a member of the oval circle. That wasn't altogether true. Actually, it wasn't true at all. It wasn't an important lie, but it was a lie. Could it be that the nervous heart buzzed when the person who wore it told a lie, even just a small lie? Lark said, "You asked whether I'm a member of the group Fuller belonged to. I'm not really a full member. I'm still too young for that. You might say I'm an apprentice." The buzzing continued. Lark could hardly hear himself talk. He added, "Actually, I'm not a member at all. I just wish I had been. And my age has nothing to do with it. I don't know any more about it than what I've heard, which isn't much." The buzzing stopped. The room was quiet again.

Lark felt better. Was it possible that the nervous rubber heart just reminded the person who wore it not to say things that weren't true? Was it possible that Lark had already discovered what the nervous rubber heart was for?

Lark didn't have time to think about it, because the assistants finished the counting. They stacked the money in neat piles on the table. Each of them wrote a number on a slip of paper. They handed the slips to Fixer. He compared the numbers on the two slips. They were the same. He told one of the assistants to bring in a large briefcase to take the money away. He told the other assistant to make out a receipt and to bring it back. He stared at the piece of paper in his hand. He shook his head. He said out loud, not really to Lark, but to himself, "So much money. I didn't know Fuller had so much money. He kept it right in his house where anyone could steal it. That's terrible. And to trust a stranger, with no receipt. That's terrible too. I don't want to insult you, Lark. But you can see it's terrible." Lark said, "I can certainly see that it looks terrible to you. But remember, Fuller was a magician. He may have had different ideas. The way he looked at it, it may not have been terrible at all." Fixer shook his head, and muttered, "I didn't understand him when he was alive. I still don't understand him now he's dead. But I'm sure of one thing. He was a good man." Lark said, "There you are. We agree completely."

The assistant came back with a piece of paper. Fixer read it carefully. He signed it, handed it to Lark, and said, "Here's your receipt. What do you want me to do with the money?" Lark said, "Put it into the bank for now. Come to Fuller's house on Sunday at five o'clock. Bring the papers Fuller signed. Make sure that Leada, Seeker and Lily are there. At that time, I'll tell everyone what I've decided, and I'll tell you what to do with the money."

Lark went to the furniture company. He found Leada in her office. He asked, "How're you doing?" Leada said, "Everyone says they can't believe he's gone. Actually, he isn't gone. Just look around you. He's everywhere, in the furniture, in the words we use, in the rules we live by. I'm doing all right, but I'll miss him." Lark asked, "And what are your plans?" Leada said, "I have no plans. We never talked about what he wanted to happen if he died. Perhaps the company will now belong to Seeker and me. I haven't had the job of running it for very long. I'm young for the job. But if he hasn't arranged for someone else to run it, I'll go on running it."

Lark asked, "And what about the house?" Leada said, "Seeker and I grew up in that house. We like it. But I'm married now. We have our own house. I can't imagine Seeker wanting to live in the house. I guess it'll have to be sold. That's sad, but that's how it is."

Lark asked, "And where is Seeker?" Leada said, "I imagine he's at the library. That's where he spends all his time. He's writing. Seeker and I were always close. We're twins, you know. But he hasn't told me what he's doing, and I didn't ask him. He'll tell me when he's ready." Lark asked, "And where's Lily?" Leada said, "Her office is right down the hall."

Lark stopped by to see Lily. He asked, "How're you doing?" Lily said, "He warned me. He said he would have to go away. I didn't understand what he meant. He was so strong. He was so healthy. We went up a mountain." Lark asked, "Are you sorry now?" Lily said, "How can you ask such a question? I'm very, very sad that he isn't here anymore. But Fuller was the most wonderful man in the world. The time I spent with him was the most wonderful time of my life. How could I be sorry?" Lark said, "But it was only three days." Lily said, "I'm surprised at you, Lark. I would have thought you'd understand. Don't you remember what Oaker said? It doesn't matter whether it's three days or thirty years. The only thing that matters is how you fill the time. For me, it was an entire life."

Lark got to the library late in the afternoon. He found Seeker in the big reading room. The room was almost empty. Seeker was sitting at a long table. There were books all around him. When he saw Lark, he stopped writing. Lark said, "I didn't want to disturb you." Seeker said, "That's all right. I'm just finishing for the day." Lark said, "In that case, why don't we go for a walk." Seeker said, "That sounds good to me. I've been sitting here all day."

They went down to the river. Lark asked, "How're you doing?" Seeker said, "I feel very bad that he'll never see it." Lark asked, "What?" Seeker said, "The book I'm making. I was doing it for him." Lark asked, "What do you mean for him?" Seeker said, "I wanted him to read what I've figured out about the world. I wanted him to be proud of me." Lark said, "He was very proud of you." Seeker said, "How do you know?" Lark said, "He told me. He said, 'Just wait until people read what Seeker has figured out about the world.'" Lark thought the nervous heart would buzz. But it didn't. Seeker said, "I never told him what I've figured out. I wanted him to read it. I wanted him to be surprised." Lark said, "He was a very wise man. He understood this. He said, he was sure what you've figured out is important, because you were waiting to finish it before talking about it. He said he was very proud of you." The nervous heart still didn't buzz. Seeker turned away. He didn't cry. But there were tears in his eyes. He said, "Maybe he knew. Thank you for telling me, Lark."

Lark asked, "And where are you going to live now?" Seeker answered, "First I'm going back to school. I'll be there next year. After that, maybe they'll make me a professor. If they do, I'll stay there. It's also possible I'll go to different places in the world." Lark asked, "And the house? Don't you want to live in the house?" Seeker said, "Leada and I grew up in the house. We like the house. We remember many things that happened there. But she is married now and has her own house. And I'll be going away. So the house will have to be sold. This makes me sad. But this is how it'll have to be."

Next morning, Lark went back to Shrinker's office. Shrinker asked, "What brings you back?" Lark said, "I know what the nervous heart is for." Shrinker was surprised. He said, "You do? So soon?" Lark said, "That's right." Shrinker said, "Are you sure? Remember, you get only one chance." Lark said, "That's all right. I'm sure." Shrinker said, "All right. Tell me."

Lark said, "Sometimes we do things that are right. Sometimes we do things that are wrong. What is right and what is wrong depends on the person. Something can be right for one person and wrong for another. Sometimes we do something wrong and don't know it's wrong, or don't want to know. But our heart always knows. When that happens our heartbeat changes. Most of the time, we're too busy, or too careless, or too frightened, or too greedy to listen. The nervous rubber heart picks up the change and buzzes.

"At first, I thought the nervous rubber heart buzzes when we say something that isn't true. It buzzed when I told Fixer I was a member of the oval circle. I said this to impress Fixer. I said it because I was vain. That was wrong, so the rubber heart buzzed. But I said to Seeker that his father told me he was proud of him. Fuller never told me anything about Seeker. But it wasn't wrong to tell Seeker that he had. So the rubber heart didn't buzz."

Shrinker came out from behind his desk, and said, "You've done well. Fuller knew what he was doing. In the old days, we would have invited you to join the oval circle." He gave Lark a hug.

On Sunday, Lark and Maya went to Fuller's house at five o'clock. Fixer, Leada, Leada's husband, and Lily were sitting in the living room when Lark and Maya arrived. Seeker was late. While they were waiting for him, Lark talked to Fixer. He told him what to do with the money. He told him what to say.

When Seeker and his girlfriend came, Lark went into the kitchen and asked Beava and Gobbler to come into the living room, and to sit down. Fixer said, "I have asked you all to come today to hear Fuller's last wishes. Lark will tell you about them. Everything Lark tells you is legal. Fuller signed all the legal papers."

Lark said, "Fuller knew that he would die right after the dinner to which he had invited us. Before we sat down to dinner, he took me aside. He gave me a message for each of you. He asked me to talk to you today. So I am going to tell you his wishes.

"Beava and Gobbler, you have had jobs in this house, and you have lived here from the time the house was built. Fuller wanted you to keep your jobs, and to go on living here, for as long as you want. Fixer has a sum of money for each of you. He is holding it in your name. He'll pay you the same salary Fuller paid you, for as long as you want to stay. When you decide to leave, you'll get the money. If the house is sold, the new owner will have to keep you as long as you want to stay.

"Seeker, your father knew that the most important thing in your life is to write down what you've figured out about the world. He wanted you to go on and make your book. He thought you'll be successful. He thought you might become famous someday. He thought you should keep your mind entirely on your work. Fixer has a large sum of money for you. He's holding it in your name. He'll send you each month double the amount Fuller has been sending you. He'll do this until you're thirty years old. At that time, you'll get all of the money.

"Leada, you are working in the furniture company. You are the boss of the company. Fuller wanted you to own the company. It is yours. Fixer is making up the legal papers." Leada said, "The furniture company was very important to Fuller. I think it should belong to both my brother and me." Lark said, "I thought so too, and I asked Fuller about it. Fuller said, I like both my daughter and my son very much. I like them equally. But they are different people. Leada is a businesswoman. She should own the company. Seeker is a philosopher. He should have enough money to live anywhere he wants, any way he wants, so he can devote all his energy to his work. That is why Fuller gave Seeker money, and gave you the company.

"Lily, Fuller told me that if he had lived, he would have asked you to marry him." Lily said, "Really?" Lark said, "Absolutely." Lily started to cry, and said, "This means a lot to me." Lark continued, "If Fuller had married you, this would have been your house too. He wanted you to have the house." Lily cried out, "No. This isn't fair. The house belongs to Leada and Seeker. I'm just a stranger. Fuller only knew me for three days." Lark said, "Remember what Oaker said. Those three days were very important to Fuller. He told me they were the days that completed his life. He hoped you would want to live in the house. But if you don't, you're free to sell the house anytime." Lily said, "I wouldn't sell Fuller's house." Lark continued, "Fuller also said you should find a nice young man, marry, and have children, If you have a boy, you should name him after Fuller." Lily cried again.

Leada said, "Our father was a wise man. This way, the house won't be sold to strangers. And I'll be able to come and visit." She hugged Lily. Seeker said, "Fuller always surprised us. Even now he's gone, he's still surprising us. And the surprising things he did always turned out well." He hugged Lily.

Fixer shook his head, and said, "I've been a lawyer for many years, but I've never seen anything like this." Lark said, "It worked, didn't it?" Fixer said, "That's what's so amazing. It wasn't supposed to work, but it did."

When Lark and Maya got home, Maya said to Lark, "I was with you every moment from the time we got to Fuller last Sunday. There was no time when Fuller could have talked to you." Lark said, "That's right." Maya said, "So it wasn't really true that Fuller told you all these things?" Lark said, "That depends on how you look at it." Maya asked, "How should I look at it?" Lark said, "Did he really tell me in those particular words? No he didn't. But he did tell me. On the Thursday before he died, he wrote me a letter. He didn't need to do that. He was with Fixer. He could have given him a full legal paper. He could have written down exactly what to give to whom. But he didn't. Why not? He wasn't a foolish man who wanted someone else to tell him what to do. He wasn't a weak man who couldn't make up his mind. He must have had some other reason. Maybe he felt that he didn't know enough about what his children wanted. Maybe he was wise enough to consider that things might happen to him in his last three days. So he asked me to decide for him after he was gone."

Maya said, "But you said he told you what to say." Lark said, "He really did, didn't he? He trusted me to figure out what he would have wanted to say, and to say it for him. That's what I did." Maya said, "But you didn't tell them that." Lark said, "There was no point in telling them. It might have made them feel bad. They might have thought their father had turned things over to a stranger. He really didn't. Fuller believed I would be able to help him do what he wanted to do. And I did."

Maya said, "By just making it up? Surely, Fuller never said Lily should name a boy after him." Lark said, "True. But he would have wanted Lily to live a normal life. He would have wanted her to marry and have children. What I told her will help her remember this." Maya said, "And what if it wasn't the right thing to tell her?" Lark said, "I was wearing the nervous rubber heart. If I had been wrong, the heart would have warned me. It didn't warn me. I did the right thing. I think Fuller wanted me to give the nervous rubber heart to Leada when I no longer needed it. I gave it to her before we left." Maya asked, "And what makes you think you didn't need it anymore?" Lark said, "The nervous rubber heart helps us listen to our heart. When we can do this on our own, we don't need the nervous rubber heart anymore."

Made in the USA
Lexington, KY
06 June 2013